YOU SHALL KNOW THEM

by **VERCORS**

THE SILENCE OF THE SEA

THREE SHORT NOVELS
  Guiding Star
  Night and Fog
  The Verdun Press

YOU SHALL KNOW THEM

YOU SHALL KNOW THEM

by **VERCORS**

TRANSLATED BY RITA BARISSE

Little, Brown and Company · *Boston*

*Published simultaneously
in Canada by McClelland and Stewart Limited*

PRINTED IN THE UNITED STATES OF AMERICA BY
KINGSPORT PRESS, INC., KINGSPORT, TENNESSEE

All man's troubles arise from the fact that we do not know what we are and do not agree on what we want to be.

— D. M. TEMPLEMORE
(Plus ou moins bête)

YOU SHALL KNOW THEM

Chapter 1

WHICH OPENS ACCORDING TO THE RULES WITH
THE DISCOVERY OF A CORPSE, SMALL BUT DISCON-
CERTING. DR. FIGGINS'S ANGER AND AMAZEMENT,
INSPECTOR BROWN'S PERPLEXITY. THE MURDERER
IS TIRESOMELY INSISTENT ON BEING CHARGED.
FIRST APPEARANCE OF THE *Paranthropus.*

OF course, to be awakened at five in the morning doesn't
exactly stir one's sense of humor — not even a doctor's.
We cannot, therefore, be surprised that Dr. Figgins, called
out as he was at crack of dawn, did not take things as we
would after a comfortable breakfast in bed. Even the
dramatic look on Douglas Templemore's face — for you
or me a reason more to chuckle over this whole comedy
of errors — was for Dr. Figgins a reason more for gloom.
So, too, was the peculiar nature of the corpse he was
shown. For this story, naturally, starts with a corpse. I
apologize for so trite an opening, but it is not my fault.

Anyway, it was only a very small corpse. And certainly
Dr. Figgins's career had afforded him ample opportunity
for meeting corpses, both large and small. So at first this

3

particular one caused him no surprise. He merely bent over the cot for a moment and then, straightening himself, fastened on Douglas a gaze in which professional sternness mingled with his best coffinside manner: his face puckered into an artistic network of wrinkles, expressing at once gravity, tact, blame and compassion. He maintained this eloquent silence for some time before announcing through the bristles of his heavy mustache:

"You've called me in a little late, I fear . . ."

Which reminded him, with a sting of resentment, of the early hour. Douglas nodded. His voice was expressionless:

"Quite so, doctor. That's what I wanted you to establish."

"I beg your pardon?"

"The child's been dead for half an hour or so, I suppose?"

Dr. Figgins thereupon forgot the hour and all the rest. His mustache swayed under a positive gale of indignation.

"Then why, in heaven's name, did you not call me sooner?"

"I'm afraid you did not understand me, doctor," said Douglas. "I gave him a shot of strychnine chlorhydrate."

Dr. Figgins recoiled a step, and knocked over a chair which he tried to retrieve as, unable to help himself, he foolishly cried:

"But . . . but that's — murder!"

"Don't doubt it."

"But what the dev . . . why . . . how could you . . .?"

"If you don't mind, doctor, I'll keep my explanations till later."

4

"I must notify the police!" the doctor declared, much agitated.

"I was going to ask you to."

Figgins took the receiver with a hand that shook a little. He rang up the Guildford police, asked for the inspector; in a voice that had meanwhile recovered its firmness, he requested him to come at once to Sunset Cottage where, he said, a crime had been committed against the person of a newborn baby.

"Infanticide?"

"Yes. The father's already admitted everything."

"Good heavens! Don't let him get away, doctor!"

"No . . . yes . . . well, he doesn't seem to want to."

He hung up and went back to the child. He lifted its eyelids, opened its mouth. He gazed with slight surprise at the small lobeless ears that were set unusually high, but he did not seem to give them much thought, for he said nothing.

Instead he opened his bag and carefully collected a drop of the child's saliva on a swab of cotton. This he placed in a small box. Then he closed his bag and sat down. Douglas had already been sitting for some time. Thus they remained in silence until the police arrived.

The inspector was a shy, courteous man with flaxen hair and beautiful manners. He interrogated Douglas with gentle deference. After the usual caution, he asked:

"You are the father, I gather?"

"I am."

"Your wife's upstairs?"

"Yes. I can call her if you like."

"Oh no," the inspector hastened to assure him. "I

5

wouldn't ask her to get up in *her* condition! I'll go and see her presently."

"I'm afraid you are under a misapprehension," said Douglas. "The child is not hers . . ."

The inspector's pale eyelids flickered a little. It took him a moment to grasp it.

"Oh . . . ah . . . well . . . is the — er — the mother here, then?"

"No," said Douglas.

"Ah . . . where is she?"

"She was taken back to the Zoo yesterday."

"The Zoo? Does she work there?"

"No. She lives there."

The inspector's eyes goggled.

"I beg your pardon?"

"The mother is not a woman, properly speaking. She is a female of the species *Paranthropus erectus*."

For a moment the doctor and the policeman gaped at Douglas without uttering a sound. Then they furtively exchanged an uneasy glance.

Douglas could not help smiling.

"If the doctor," he suggested, "cares to examine the child a little more closely, he will doubtless be struck by certain anomalies."

Only for a second did the doctor hesitate. Then he strode over to the cot, uncovered the little body, and removed the diaper.

He simply said, "Damn!" and furiously seized his hat and bag.

This brought the inspector to his side with anxious speed.

6

"What's the matter, doctor?"

"This isn't a boy," barked Dr. Figgins. "It's a monkey."

"Are you sure?" asked Douglas in an odd voice.

Figgins grew very red in the face.

"What do you mean, am I sure! Inspector," he said, "we've been the victims of a stupid hoax. I don't know what you propose doing, but I for my part . . ."

He did not bother to finish the sentence: he was already making for the door.

"Just a minute, doctor, if you don't mind," Douglas intervened, in a voice that brooked no denial. He held out to him a sheet of paper that he had taken from a drawer in his desk. The paper bore the heading of the Australian College of Surgeons. "Will you read this?"

After a moment's hesitation the doctor took the paper and put on his spectacles. He read:

I hereby certify that this day at 4:30 A.M. I have delivered a pithecoid female, known as Derry, of the species *Paranthropus erectus,* of a male child in sound physical condition; and that the said birth took place as a result of an artificial insemination carried out by me in Sydney on December 9, 19— for the purpose of scientific investigation, the donor being Douglas M. Templemore.

SELBY D. WILLIAMS, M.D., K.B.E.

Dr. Figgins's naturally globular eyes bulged behind their spectacles to surprising dimensions. "He's going to lay them like eggs . . . " Douglas thought. Without a word, the doctor handed the document to the inspector, glared at Douglas as though he were the ghost of Cromwell, and walked back to the cot.

"Never heard of such a thing!" he muttered dully. "What is this . . . this *Paranthropus?*"

"Nobody knows yet."

"What do you mean?"

"A sort of anthropoid. Some thirty of them have just arrived in this country. They're being studied at the moment."

"But what have you . . ." the doctor began, but broke off and turned back to the cot.

"It's a monkey all the same. It's four-handed." There was a note of relief in his voice.

"That's rather jumping to conclusions," said Douglas mildly.

"There are no four-handed human beings."

"Doctor," said Douglas, "suppose, for instance, that a railway accident . . . look, let's cover up the legs. There, a little corpse with the feet gone. Would you be quite so categorical?"

There was a pause.

"His arms are too long," the doctor said at last.

"But his face?"

The doctor raised his eyes in a helpless perplexity that bordered on a panic.

"His ears . . ." he began.

"And suppose," said Douglas, "that in a few years' time we'd manage to teach him to read, write and reckon?"

"You can suppose anything you like since we'll never know," said Figgins hastily, with a shrug.

"Perhaps we shall. He has brothers, doctor. Two have already been born at the Zoo, by other females. Three more soon will be."

8

"Time enough then," stammered the doctor, wiping his forehead.

"Time to what?"

"To . . . to see . . . to know . . ."

The inspector drew nearer. His pale eyelashes were fluttering like moths.

"Mr. Templemore, what exactly do you expect us to do?"

"Your job, Inspector."

"But what job, sir? This little creature is a monkey, that's plain. Why the dickens do you want to . . ."

"That's my business, Inspector."

"Well, ours is certainly not to meddle . . ."

"I have killed my child, Inspector."

"I've grasped that. But this . . . this creature isn't a . . . it doesn't present . . ."

"He's been christened, Inspector, and his birth duly entered at the registry office under the name of Garry Ralph Templemore."

Fine beads of perspiration broke out on the inspector's face. He suddenly shot a question at Douglas.

"Under what name was the mother entered?"

"Under her own, Inspector: 'Native woman from New Guinea, known as Derry.'"

"False declaration!" cried the inspector triumphantly. "The whole registration is invalid."

"False declaration?"

"The mother isn't a woman."

"That remains to be proved."

"Why, you yourself — "

"Opinions are divided."

9

"Divided? Divided about what? Whose opinions?"

"Those of the leading anthropologists, about the species the *Paranthropus* belongs to. It's an intermediate species: man or ape? It resembles both. It may well be that Derry is a woman after all. It's up to you to prove the contrary, if you can. In the meantime her child is my son, before God and the law."

The inspector seemed so disconcerted that Douglas took pity on him.

"Perhaps," he suggested kindly, "you would like to refer the matter to your chief?"

The tow-colored face brightened.

"Yes, if you don't mind, sir."

The inspector lifted the receiver and asked for Guildford. He could not help flashing a grateful smile towards the murderer.

The doctor drew a few steps closer.

"But then," he said, "if I've understood you rightly . . . you're going to find yourself father of five more little monkeys, just like this one?"

"You're beginning to understand, doctor," said Douglas.

Chapter 2

WHICH ADDS, AS IS PROPER, TO A SPOT OF CRIME,
A SPRINKLING OF LOVE. INTRODUCTION TO
FRANCES DORAN IN HER SMALL VILLAGE IN THE
HEART OF LONDON. INTRODUCTION TO DOUGLAS
TEMPLEMORE IN THE ATMOSPHERE OF THE
PROSPECT OF WHITBY. THEY MEET, AS IT HAP-
PENS, NEITHER HERE NOR THERE, BUT AMID THE
FLOWERING DAFFODILS.

I<small>T</small> all started on a lovely April morning (London's climate is grossly maligned) while Frances Doran was strol-
ling in Regent's Park, over the greensward dotted with
daffodils. She was walking amid a transparent mist that
the sun drew up in wisps from the sparkling grass. She
had a deep affection for this park, a very special love.
Which was odd for someone who lived surrounded by the
trees and fields of another sort of park: the one that,
farther north, overhangs the vast city and is called Hampstead Heath — the largest and wildest of London's open
spaces. If you come towards it from the south, your road
at first skirts an expanse of patchy grass which the famous

11

fair, held there periodically, has trodden almost bare. You pass a few side streets, one of which sheltered for a while the too brief candle of John Keats's life; then, as the road begins to climb, the whole Heath stretches away to the right, with its green slopes and woods and dells that seem miles away from the crowded city. If halfway up the hill you now take a narrow road that winds gently down between the trees, you will find at the bottom, nestling in its green hiding place, a diminutive village, whose unexpected presence amid London's ocean of bricks and stones is the most touching thing in the world. It goes by the promising name of the Vale of Health, which may contain a touch of irony since fog and mist (by all accounts) love to linger there. But the day on which I discovered it was, of course, a sunny one. . . . The girl who accompanied me, though a Londoner, was discovering it with me, and we both felt a thrill of excitement. For it really *was* a village, with its cottages, narrow lanes, village green, and even a pub standing beside a misty pond. We walked through one of those lanes just wide enough for two people walking abreast, and I well remember that we noticed a small house standing back in its doll's-sized garden, its timbered upper story covered by wistaria and Virginia creeper. A wide bay on the ground floor opened on to a tiny garden, and revealed to the passer-by who had strayed into this improbable hamlet a cosy interior furnished with graceful but striking simplicity. Seeing no one in it, we dawdled outside, never guessing that this little house, snuggling in the heart of a forgotten village in the heart of a heath in the heart of London would one day be singled out for fame.

12

For it was here that Frances lived. I have no idea whether the house had come to her from her parents or whether fortune had smiled on her. She lived alone and seldom went out, for she was happy there writing those tales and short stories which the literary monthlies printed without much eagerness, and the publishers collected in book form with even less. She had, however, some faithful admirers, whose fervor and sincerity hardly compensated for their lack of numbers.

She was thus frequently assailed by self-doubts and overdrafts. And say what you will, neither of them is of much use in reducing the other. At times this would affect her writing. Which did not help matters either. At others, though, these very trials would quicken her courage and sharpen her vision; and, reading her stories, her unknown admirers, too few and far away, would feel a warm surge of excitement, and they would have liked to know her.

Douglas, too, lived by his pen. But his particular line was factual reporting. He had a knack of discovering groups of human oddities whose strange lives he described with a vivid turn of phrase. He had, for example, unearthed in Devonshire a brotherhood of old retired majors all firmly vowed to singleness. Some thirty of them were living in an ancient, tumble-down manor house haunted by a profusion of ghosts. His account of their eccentric way of life had set even the somewhat snobbish readers of *Horizon* chortling with amused affection.

Impossible to describe the house Douglas lived in as accurately as Frances's. Not that I haven't seen it, or if not his very house at least five hundred like it: but that's

13

precisely what blights my descriptive vein. There are few more melancholy sights than London's endless rows of uniform houses under their coat of soot and desolation. Douglas claims that his choice of Caribbean Street, that squalid East End Road in the depths of dockland, was prompted by his taste for atmosphere. The truth is that, as a young writer, he had had quite a struggle to keep the wolf from the door. But it is indeed probable that he later grew attached to that vast waterside slum with its medley of gaiety, tenderness, crime, patience and despair, and its river that is a gateway to the whole world. However that may be, certain tyrannical habits now bound him to the place. Every night at seven he would go and have a drink at the Prospect of Whitby, a local pub overflowing with curiosities. At that hour you cannot squeeze a sardine into it. Except for a table by the door and a long bench at the back, there is nowhere to sit. Everybody stands around, glass in hand, as tightly wedged as in rush hours in the underground, and everybody drinks and smokes and talks and sings while the sound of two old Hawaiians scraping their mewing guitars is relayed by a loud-speaker that deafens the narrow room. Behind the bar, among innumerable bottles and stuffed fishes, hangs a fantastic collection of indescribable junk. Leaving out of account the ships in bottles, the compasses, sextants, ships' bells, and other seafaring odds and ends, there is everything here that popular imagination can devise for its own amusement: flowers made of paper, of shells, feathers, bone, glass, velvet, silk, hair, cellophane; vases shaped like feet with corns on each toe, or like fat red heads, or long green ones; little *mannequin-pisse* scent-

14

sprays; pumpkin teapots, teapot lanterns, lanterns like calves' heads with china parsley in each nostril; old shoes made of licorice; marzipan nudes with chaste petticoats of crimped paper. . . . Douglas had never been able to analyze the mysterious spell that drew him night after night to this place where man's loving delight in the things he makes mingles with the singing and the smoke. He was constantly fascinated by a mummified Red Indian head, shriveled to the size of a baby's fist but still flaunting its proud sheaf of hair. He had often thought of asking the barkeeper to sell it to him, but he had never dared, held back by a natural shyness that his profession had failed to quench. Perhaps it was as well: he would certainly have met with a rebuff. So he would drink and look at it while behind the bar, amid the lights and the clatter of glasses, the landlord and his staff would bustle about: two bartenders and two barmaids for the customers crowding the narrow wooden balcony at the far end of a dark passage. From this balcony Henry VIII, it seems, used to watch the hangings on the gallows across the river. Its old, grease-encrusted timbers, carved with innumerable names, overhang the Thames at a point where two wrecks lie rotting in the mud. Just below it a dark, forbidden alley that runs alongside the pub ends in a worm-eaten, wooden stairway leading down to the water. At night, only the topmost steps are feebly lighted by a baleful gas lamp standing at the alley's entrance; and you cannot help imagining the corpse of many a murdered person being dragged of old down those battered steps, to be swallowed up in the evil-gleaming inkiness below.

But it was in the April sunshine of Regent's Park, amid

15

the daffodils and the morning mist, that Douglas met Frances. Not that this meeting was really so very surprising: Douglas shared the girl's love for this flowery park. They had probably passed each other a number of times without paying any heed. Why was it different this morning?

No doubt because of the mist and the sun. The silhouette of Frances bending over the daffodils may have looked somewhat ghostly, but it was certainly charming. She was bareheaded and her fair burnished hair gleamed softly in the thin mist. Douglas could not make out her features. He felt he would have liked to. He stopped. The girl raised her head and saw a veritable eclipse of the sun: a black disk of a face lighted from behind and surrounded by copper-colored flames that swayed in the wind. She could not help smiling. Douglas took the smile as a personal tribute, and since the girl was beautiful, even though her mouth was a little large, he felt a warm gratitude for that smile, and his heart went out to her loveliness. Moreover, the smile encouraged him.

"What wonderful flowers!" he said.

But Frances understood quite well that he meant "What a pretty face!" and though she was aware of her own beauty his remark pleased her. She smiled again, but this time out of friendliness.

"You like them?" she asked.

He came nearer and sat on the grass, cross-legged, and gazed at her. "Immensely," he said, but she cried:

"You'll catch a cold!"

He jumped up, saying, "How nice of you," and he took off his raincoat and spread it out. He ostentatiously

16

sat down on one end of it so that she, with hardly a moment's hesitation, sat down quite naturally on the other. He smiled broadly and announced:

"This *is* a piece of luck!"

She raised her eyebrows.

"Our having met," he said. "Once in a while a glorious day like this comes along: full of flowers and sunshine and the smile of young girls."

"I'm twenty-nine, you know," she said. (She was thirty.)

"You look half."

She laughed without constraint. She felt full of joy. A boat passed with a fat lady in it, rowed by a boy who was straining at the overheavy oars.

"I've nothing to do till noon," Douglas ventured to say. "What about you?"

"I've nothing to do till next year."

"What! As free as all that?"

"As a mountain goat. I work when I feel like it."

"And you won't feel like it till next year?"

"I can't tell. Perhaps I shall presently. Perhaps never."

"What do you do? Paint?"

"No. Write."

"*Sans blague!*" he cried.

"Why '*sans blague*'?"

"Because I write too."

And off they went. The talk that followed isn't worth reporting. When two writers begin to talk shop it's of no interest to anyone except writers.

At the end of an hour they began to feel cold. They got up, still talking. Frances quite well remembered the

17

article in *Horizon* about the majors. Douglas felt contrite at not having read anything of hers; but when, at his request, she began enumerating the stories she had written, and mentioned the one in which two married people, all by themselves in a lonely mountain chalet in the snow, spend their long winter evenings sulking at opposite ends of the house, he cried: "What, *you* wrote that?" and showed frank excitement. Which warmed her heart. They soon noticed that it was long past noon. With a wave of his arm Douglas sent his appointment to blazes, and they sat down to lunch in a Chinese restaurant in Soho, where they absent-mindedly ordered cress sandwiches, hard-boiled eggs and synthetic mayonnaise.

တ

A little later they took the bus to Hampstead Heath on their way to the Vale of Health. Douglas was amazed — and a trifle mortified: he had known of the existence of this curious village, of course, but he had never been there. How could he have missed such a place until that day? Frances laughed with childish vanity. They ambled through the little streets before entering her house. There they lighted a log fire in the small cherry-wood fireplace, and while he settled down on the floor, pipe in mouth, his knees up to his chin and his arms clasping his limp flannels, she made some tea without interrupting their talk.

When dusk fell he reluctantly rose to go. But she made him stay, and for dinner opened tins of English peas and sliced pineapple. At ten o'clock, though, she let him go. "Well, so I'm in love," he thought to himself, on top of

18

the bus on the way home, as the few lights still burning in Fleet Street went flashing by. It wasn't the first time, but there was something novel in this love, something warm and peaceful. The end of a verse by Verlaine — a poet he knew by heart — kept running through his head: ". . . *sans redouter d'embûche* . . ."* He did not even ask himself whether he had any chance of being loved in return.

* ". . . without fear of pitfalls . . ."

Chapter 3

WHEREIN FRANCES AND DOUGLAS BOTH PRO-
CLAIM THE SUPERIORITY OF FRIENDSHIP OVER
LOVE. THE CONVENIENCE OF LITERATURE IN
THIS RESPECT. THE INCONVENIENCE OF SILENCE.
DANGERS OF SMILES. DOUGLAS'S PANIC AND IM-
PRUDENCE. FRANCES DORAN'S IMPRUDENCE AND
WRATH. HOW GREAT DECISIONS COME TO BE
TAKEN. THREE TEETH ON A MANDIBLE SEAL A
DOUBLE FATE. LITERATURE LEADS TO ANYTHING
PROVIDED YOU TURN YOUR BACK ON IT.

THEY saw each other almost every day. It was always at
her place. He would come towards five, take off the jacket
that covered his thick crimson sweater, and squat down
in front of the fire which she had lighted for him. He
would fill his pipe, and she would serve tea with matzoth
crackers bought at a Jewish grocer's in Swiss Cottage.

When he didn't come, they used to write, generally
about some literary point or other that had come up during his last visit. There would always be some point under
discussion when he left. They'd also leave one or two

20

questions unsettled in their letters. So there was invariably a reason for seeing or writing each other again.

And above all, this kept the silences at bay.

For their relationship had become established on immutable lines. It was tacitly understood that they were *not* in love: *so* petty and conventional! She was thirty, he was thirty-five. Passion had ravaged their lives on two or three occasions: they were "inoculated," they said. Whereas friendship! Of course, they had plenty of friends, both of them. But none whom they could trust with that splendid abandon which was the most cherished mark of their affection. What she had always dreamed of had come to life in him: a man with brains, understanding, and a keenly critical mind, who gave her his exact opinion of her stories, frankly and without bias. What security! It was wonderful to hear him say: "That won't do," then explain why. All you had to do was tear up the pages and start again (or let them sleep for a while). And what certainty when, on the contrary, he'd exclaim: "Grand!" Whereas previously her friends had gurgled over everything she wrote, "Divine, darling, quite exquisite!" and left her to the agony of trying to judge for herself. A never-ending torture!

"Thank God," she thought, "that he isn't in love with me!" And she honestly believed that she was praying heaven for it not to happen. Love, she thought, would spoil this precious sincerity. Or at least blur his judgment. And for what, I ask you? For what cheap rapture? That her own affection went perhaps a little beyond friendship, that it was tinged with tenderness, sometimes even with a sensual desire which she accepted

21

with a sweet and secret pleasure — all this held no real danger. But not he, she prayed. If only he won't think of me like that!

As for him, he had either forgotten, or pretended he had, the feelings that had stirred him on top of the bus that first evening. He still felt bruised by a betrayal that had left him not so much desperate as disgusted. Women's love, he thought, pshaw! Nauseous quagmire! They lie for our good, they say, to save us suffering. And of course you find them out, and of course you do suffer, and on top of it there is the disgust. And they despise you for your suffering and for your disgust, which show how little you appreciate the divine loving-kindness of their too-sensitive hearts. God forbid, he thought, that I should get bogged down again in a woman's love!

Whereupon he took the bus to Hampstead Heath, squeezed Frances's hands with a happy laugh, hung up his coat, lighted his pipe, and while she snuggled voluptuously into the protective cushiony depth of the divan, he would resume their talk at the point where they had last left it. And she would listen with delighted, trustful, shining eyes in which he refused to see what a child of six could have read there.

At times, however, something happened that left them ill at ease: a point would be settled, exhausted, and no other could be found at once. And then would fall one of those silences that they had come to dread. For they did not know how to fill them. They did not know how to accept them and be grateful for the simple pleasure of being together: to follow silently each his own train of thought until words came spontaneously, or even just

22

dream in the twilight, watching the flames. No, it seemed to them that if the silence persisted, it would release some catch, open the door to some telltale devil who would leave them helpless and bewildered. So they would smile at each other almost provocatively, as if to say: "Nothing to fear, is there?" until one or the other, wildly casting around, had at last fished up a new topic. But sometimes the pause would lengthen, and as they groped in panic their smile gradually hardened into a meaningless grimace. And yet neither of them dared to be the first to stop smiling, and that was really awful.

So one day, for no other reason than to break that hateful tension, Douglas blurted out:

"D'you know that the Greames want me to go with them?"

He said it without thinking, yet no sooner was it said than everything was sealed. And it was not even true.

Douglas had indeed run into Cuthbert Greame the day before, waiting for a bus in Regent Street. Old Greame had been a Cambridge friend of his father's, the Sinologist Hermon Templemore. Douglas retained a warm regard for him, for the young man had been deeply attached to his father, although they had almost quarreled when the boy wanted to strike out for himself. Greame was now sixty-five. He had the round, puffy face of an alcoholic old cabby, moist blue eyes of angelic candor, a pathetic difficulty in speaking in public (even if the public were but one man), and a knowledge of paleontology recognized by anthropologists as being unsurpassed.

He had blushed on seeing Douglas — he always

23

blushed when he met people, as if he lived in constant fear of being caught in the act. In reply to the young man's greeting he stammered:

"'Lo . . . Fine . . . And you? Good, good . . ."

He glanced right and left as if trying to escape. Douglas asked him for news of Sybil.

"She's well . . . quite well . . . that's to say . . . she's got a bout of measles, imagine . . ."

"Serves her right!" Douglas could not help thinking with a grin, and he saw himself again at thirteen, and Sybil in the doorway facing his bed, tossing back her fair curls with a pout of disgust at the sight of the youngster's pimply red face. She too was thirteen at the time. Douglas had never forgiven her that callous grimace.

At the age of twenty Sybil had married Greame, who was then fifty. People had promptly called her mercenary, and him a giddy old fool. Later, when she flew out to the Transvaal with him on his quest for the Africanthrope, and took part in the digging with marked efficiency, the wagging tongues were silenced. People confined themselves to reminding each other that her marriage had broken the heart of many an eligible young man, and especially, they said, of that nice Templemore boy.

The only one who did not know that his heart was broken was Douglas Templemore himself. That is probably why he never told Frances about it. But her friends were less discreet. She never mentioned the fact to Douglas, though: imagine her stooping to jealousy! Ridiculous.

"Measles!" said Douglas. "But that's a children's complaint!"

Greame's eyes lit for a moment with a touching tender-

24

ness. He smiled, and then flushed to the roots of his hair, his blue eyes clouded with embarrassment.

"Not always . . . not always . . . one can quite well . . . anyway, it's almost over," he said hurriedly.

With obvious relief he saw his bus coming.

"Good thing too," he ended up, "because . . . we've advanced the date of our trip. You know? New Guinea. They found there . . . here's my bus . . . a mandible . . . jawbone, y'know . . . half ape, half man. You see? . . . With three molars — but it would take too long . . ."

"How thrilling," said Douglas kindly.

"Thrilling, yes. You're interested? We'll certainly take two cameramen with us. And we're thinking of a journalist. Not for the digging, for the — "

The old scientist was swept into the bus by the stream of passengers. On the edge of the platform he waved his hand before he was swallowed from sight.

"Hope to see you," he cried.

Laughingly, amid the noise of the departing bus, he called out something more, which could have been "Don't be too long!" or "Why not come along?" and then he disappeared.

Now Douglas was flabbergasted by the news he had just announced to Frances, and which was so meagerly supported by facts. "What's come over me?" he thought, and would have corrected himself at once. But he saw Frances bounce out of her cushions like a jack-in-the-box.

"But that's wonderful!" she cried with excessive gaiety. "Absolutely wonderful! You've accepted, of course?"

She did not herself know why she spoke like that. There had been that long cramped smile, unbearable in the

25

silence, and then the panic, that sort of giddiness that always seized her. And then at last Douglas had said something, and she'd felt relief: but what he had said was *that* thing, and she felt painfully hurt.

"You think I ought to?" asked Douglas.

He looked surprised and abashed. But she felt painfully hurt. Too brightly she repeated:

"Why, of course, it's wonderful. You can't let this slip. When are they going?"

"I don't know exactly," Douglas stammered. He really looked pitiable. "In a fortnight, I suppose. . . ." So pitiable that Frances was touched for a moment. But she was hurt, she was hurt.

"You must ring them!" she cried. And gaily she went to look up the directory. "Primrose 6099," she announced and handed Douglas the telephone. The young man almost rebelled. He was going to protest, "But what's come over you?" when she said:

"You need a change of air. You've been in London far too long."

She was often to ask herself, with rage and sadness, what had driven her to say those words. It couldn't be jealousy. She didn't care a rap about that Sybil. He could go wherever he liked with her. We aren't in love, are we? We can quite well part for a while. We are free.

Douglas felt stunned. "Far too long in London!" So that was what she thought at heart. Why hadn't she said so sooner? He took the receiver and dialed the number.

It was Sybil who answered. At first she could not grasp what Douglas wanted. A journalist? She was quite aware that Douglas was a journalist! Why phone her this great news? Go with them to New Guinea? "But my dear little

Doug . . . What? You can never hear a word over the phone. Come and see me, if you're not afraid of measles. Whenever you like."

He hung up. He was looking at Frances as if he saw her through a haze. She brought him his jacket and his raincoat.

"Go and see her at once!" she said with the same overdone brightness. "Don't give them time to cool off."

They kept standing there, motionless, face to face, and she had time to think: "This is idiotic. I'm going to kiss him. It's too foolish. I won't let him go. Yes, I will, he's hurt me, it's all spoiled. Let him go, go . . . Oh, why doesn't he fling that jacket across the room and take me in his arms!"

But he thrust his arms into the sleeves of his jacket and threw the raincoat over his shoulder. Then she started pushing him towards the door.

"You've got to seize opportunity by the forelock," she said with a ringing laugh. "Even if it's a blond forelock."

He looked at Frances's blond hair. What opportunity was she talking of? Not for a second did he think of Sybil's hair. Seize what opportunity? He thought in a flash: "I'll marry her!" But no, she didn't want him in the least. Her light fingers on his arm were pushing him towards the door. Under his feet he felt the soft, friendly hall carpet. It seemed to him he could actually *see* its green and brown checks with the soles of his feet, and it filled him with such longing he could have broken down and cried.

On the doorstep she added:

"Better hurry. Take a taxi."

The tiny garden was resplendent with May flowers

under the twilight sky. Forget-me-nots, aubrietias, periwinkles, anemones and a tuft of irises with flowers more lovely than orchids. The fine gravel crunched beneath his feet.

She waved her hand as he went through the gate. "Mind you come and see me before leaving town!" she cried. In the evening light she seemed to him suffused with radiant beauty. She was smiling at him with that lovely, slightly wide, red mouth. She looked gloriously happy.

∽

"What was it Cuthbert said to you?" asked Sybil, who could not make head or tail of it all.

She was lying on a Regency couch, a fur rug over her legs. She still had some rough, reddish marks on her face — but who would have dreamed of scanning her complexion . . . when her eyes were turned on him? Douglas, however, did not think of looking at either.

"Well . . . er . . . that you need a journalist," he said, straining the truth a little. "And then he called to me: 'Won't you come with us, do!' "

"But what on earth would you do with us? Are you interested in paleontology? It doesn't deal with the same kind of fossils as your majors!"

Douglas sought for an answer. Never had he been less anxious to convince anyone.

"Everything interests me," he said mournfully.

He saw that she was studying him with quizzical eyes. He flushed.

"I say," she suggested, "you don't happen to be running away, do you? Nobody's broken your heart?"

28

"Good Lord, no," he protested, with quick annoyance. "What an idea! Really, your expedition interests me a lot. I am certain that for me, professionally speaking . . ."

"Do you at least know what we are looking for?"

He felt a fleeting panic — and then he recalled one word. He brought it out triumphantly:

"A mandible . . ."

With a grin he added:

". . . plus three teeth."

She laughed affectionately. Wasn't he sweet! She liked him a lot.

"No," she said. "The mandible and the three teeth — they were brought back by Kreps, the German geologist. What we'll try and find are the skull and the skeleton."

"That's what I meant," muttered Douglas.

"If we manage to lay hands on them, we may have discovered the so-called 'missing link.' You know what that is?"

"Yes . . . at least . . . roughly," he stuttered. "The link that's missing in the chain of evolution . . . the final link between man and the ape . . ."

"And that interests you — passionately?" she asked with mocking emphasis.

"Well, why on earth shouldn't it?"

"Because, Doug darling, you can't just drop into zoology as if it were a tea party. When I tell you that we are off to New Guinea because the third molar in Kreps's jawbone has five tubercles, does that make you jump with excitement?"

"Not if you say it like that. But I know enough to grasp that Kreps must have found a monkey tooth in a human jaw, or something of that sort. Right?"

29

"Yes, that's it, more or less."

"You see I am not a complete imbecile."

"I never said you were. I was asking you: does that make you jump with excitement?"

"But why do you want me to jump? I didn't jump either when I heard of the old majors living down at Stagford Manor. I went there and brought back my story, that's all."

"If you come with us you won't get much of a story."

"Why not?"

"Because it's obvious that you've never seen any digging of this sort. It isn't spectacular, I can assure you. You turn up some tons of earth. You sift them. At the end of six weeks, or six months, you find amid the gravel or the shells a piece of fossilized bone, or a tooth. You first make sure they couldn't have got there by accident, that they definitely are of the same age as the soil — a million years old or so. In that case, you go on with the digging. If in the months that follow you are lucky enough to hit on a piece of a skull or a thighbone you are well content. Because most of the time you won't find anything at all. You can see that this would hardly be of much interest to you."

"How can you judge what is or what isn't of interest to me?"

As he spoke, Cuthbert Greame came in. He seemed surprised to see Douglas, but genuinely pleased. He cried: "Hallo!" and shook his hand vigorously. Then he went to kiss Sybil.

"Well," said she, "the die is cast: Douglas is coming with us."

Douglas almost toppled over:

"What! But . . ."

Sybil stopped him with a gesture and a charming smile.

"I've done all I could to discourage him," she told her husband. "But, God knows why, he won't give up the idea. Have you already fixed things up with Speed?"

"Well . . . er . . . practically," stammered Greame, who felt that events were outstripping him. "I didn't know that . . . but we certainly could . . ."

"Look here — " cried Douglas.

"Leave it to me," said Sybil. "Speed wasn't so very keen to go. It was rather that he didn't want to let us down — let *me* down, more especially," she said with a smile. "In fact, I am sure he will be glad to be out of it. You know him?" she asked Douglas.

"Sort of . . . vaguely . . ." and quickly he added: "That's just why — I wouldn't on any account . . ."

"You needn't have the slightest qualms, believe me. All that Speed will do is to sigh with relief. The job's no joke, I tell you. It's keeping the logbook. None of us is much good with a pen — nor, for that matter, would we have time to keep a diary regularly: we'll have too many other things on our minds. Well," she wound up, "it's a deal. No regrets?"

He would have liked to find the courage to say: "At least give me time to think it over," but he could not get the words out: the old scientist and his wife were looking at him with such a friendly smile, so patently delighted to have pleased him. "Let's have a drink!" said Greame, and went to fetch some whisky. While he was filling their glasses, his kind, chubby red face beamed with happy affection.

31

Chapter 4

EMBARKATION FOR SUOGUARAI. FRANCES AND
DOUGLAS CONSENT TO LOVE EACH OTHER, BUT
APART. CONVENIENCE OF SILENCE. EASE OF
SMILES. INTRODUCTION ON BOARD SHIP TO A
GERMAN GEOLOGIST, AN IRISH BENEDICTINE
PRIEST AND A BRITISH ANTHROPOLOGIST. THE
LOVELY SYBIL INITIATES DOUGLAS INTO THE FEUD
OF ORTHOGENESIS VERSUS SELECTION. FROM FOS-
SIL SHELLS TO BRAIN CONVOLUTIONS. HOFMANNS-
THAL BY MOONLIGHT.

THE expedition arrived in Liverpool a few days before
they sailed, to collect their final impedimenta. Douglas
had not seen Frances again. His mind was in too much of
a turmoil. He no longer concealed from himself that he
loved her. That she too loved him seemed hardly less
certain, now that he could examine things more calmly:
the whole silly business was nothing but an idiotic misunderstanding. But what could be done now? It was impossible, in all decency, to let down the Greames, who
had released Speed for his sake. He had been to see that

fellow Speed, in a last hope that he might perhaps have liked to go. But Sybil had been right: Speed was delighted to find himself replaced.

As for Frances, he had not even dared to ring her. The thing to do, of course, would have been to rush to her, take her in his arms, and screw up the courage to bring the whole matter out into the open. He had indeed tried to make up his mind to it one evening, but after hanging around the lanes of the Vale of Health for hours, he had thought he saw her and promptly taken to his heels.

Frances, for her part, was having a wretched time. She kept on reading Douglas's letter telling her of his departure. A letter wonderfully like its predecessors, bearing the stamp of that quiet humor, sound judgment and honesty that had given Frances such confidence ever since the first day. But over the last lines she broke down:

In brief, here I am setting off against my will. But all is well if you think it is well. A word from you has made me go. A word from you would have made me stay. This obedience is hard on me, but I like to obey you. There are painful joys like that, aren't there, Frances? Whatever comes to me from you will always be a joy, even pain. My dear, don't abuse this, please. Good-by. Think of me sometimes.

Yours ever,

DOUGLAS

And then, on the day they sailed, just as Douglas, at the third hoot of the siren, had gone on deck with a

33

heavy heart, at least to watch the English coast passing out of sight, he had suddenly recognized among the people on the quayside, a motionless silhouette that had made him catch his breath. "Frances!" he shouted, and rushed to the gangway. Too late: it had already been raised. He raced back astern. Frances had come quite close to the edge. Douglas saw the lovely, slightly pallid face lifted towards him. They found nothing to say — no doubt because they would have had to shout. Frances simply smiled, he returned the smile. And for the first time the silence could last an unbelievable while without their being gripped by panic. And their smile grew more natural, more lighthearted, every moment. Frances raised her hand a little, brought it to her lips, and Douglas did the same. And without ceasing to smile they waved their fingers until the ship had disappeared beyond the mole.

ᔕᕼ

Douglas hoped to use the long voyage for getting a little more familiar with paleontology. But he was disappointed. His companions seemed to have but one care: never to talk shop.

There were three men and Sybil. It took Douglas weeks to grasp the special line of each of them. The biggest surprise was to learn that the hard-drinking, heavy-eating old pipe smoker with a penchant for broad language was an Irish Benedictine father. Douglas had indeed heard him called Pop all day long, but he had never thought that this nickname could be due to anything other than his age.

"You can't get away from it: it always shows through,"

34

Sybil had said one night (they were passing Socotora Island), as the curly white head was fading away along the promenade deck. They were both stretched out in deck chairs.

"What does?" asked Douglas.

"The cloth," said Sybil, who enjoyed professing a scandalous atheism.

"What cloth?"

"Why, the cleric's."

Douglas's surprise must have been comical, to judge by the laughter it aroused.

"What! You didn't know? Not only is he a papist, but a Benedictine to boot; and worst of all, he's a rabid orthogenetist."

"A what?"

"An orthogenetist. A supporter of orthogenesis. He believes that evolution has an aim. At least, a direction."

The expression of Douglas's face was pathetic. With some exasperation Sybil explained:

"He thinks that mutations don't happen by accident, by natural selection, but that they are purposive, directed: that they obey an urge towards self-perfection . . . Oh hell!" she burst out, faced with that persistent blankness, "He thinks there's a plan and a planner. That God knows beforehand what He is after," she summed up.

"That's not a crime," said Douglas with a smile.

"No. It's poppycock."

"And what are you?"

"Huh?"

"If you aren't an orthogenetist, what *are* you?"

"Nothing. I haven't lined up. I think orthogenesis is

35

mystical eyewash. I hold with Darwin that natural selection plays a main part, but I don't think it's the whole story. That evolution is the result of complex factors, internal and external — all sorts of interdependencies. I think it'll never be possible to reduce evolution to a single factor. I think those who do are donkeys."

"Tell me — the external features, they're climate, food, other animals?"

"Yes."

"And selection — that means that the forms best adapted to those factors survive and flourish? While the less adaptable ones die out?"

"Roughly."

"And the internal factors?"

"They are the forces of transformation that spring from a sort of collective will of the species, a common urge towards self-improvement."

"An urge to become more and more like . . . some ideal prototype, in effect?"

"Yes, let's put it like that."

"And you believe in both factors at the same time?"

"I do: and in others as well. A lot of others, less explicable."

"For instance?"

"I can't explain them since they are not explicable."

"Of a divine nature?"

"Heavens, no. Not at all. Beyond the reach of human intelligence, that's all."

"And you believe in them without understanding them?"

"I cannot conceive what their nature is since there's

36

no way of knowing them. I believe that they exist, that's all."

"But that's of no use, then."

"What d'you mean?"

"It's pretty much like believing in Santa Claus."

She laughed and stared at him with a new respect.

"That's not so dumb, what you said."

"I think I would rather hold on to what my mind can grasp. To natural selection and to ... to ... hormogenesis, for instance."

"*Ortho*genesis. That would be reasonable enough. But there are things which even the two together cannot account for.

"For example?"

"For example, the sudden extinction of certain species in their prime. Or else, quite simply, the human brain."

"Why the human brain?"

"That would take too long to explain. Let's say, broadly speaking, you knock up against too many contradictions. If our brain power is simply there to promote the biological welfare of the human species — why then does our brain gratuitously meddle at the same time with something quite different? And if it's a matter of that 'something different,' well, in that case, it's a gigantic flop."

"Perhaps we're only at the first chapter."

"Well, that's what I'm saying: when we come to the last chapter we may understand the causes."

"Shall I tell you something?"

"What?"

"At bottom you're even more orthogenetical than Pop."

37

"That's a sentimental judgment, Doug, my dear."

"Sentimental?"

"Even Pop is an orthogenetist only for strictly scientific reasons — at least, he's convinced of it. It's not because he believes in a divine will that he's an orthogenetist: but because he's an orthogenetist he believes in a divine will. And he's an orthogenetist only because . . . because of the way — among other things — that certain types of fossil shells are coiled up. He's found some variations of the species where coiling has gone so far that the creature eventually died shut up inside its own shell while still quite young. And yet, those species have survived in spite of this obstacle. Whence Pop infers the existence of an internal factor, an inner 'will to coil,' contrary to all adaptive processes. To which Cuthbert replies, as a stanch Darwinist, that the internal factor was originally nothing more than an adaptive process that had got out of hand in the course of genetic development. They've been quarreling like fishwives about it for the last three years."

"Because your husband is keen on shells, too?"

"My dear Douglas, if you want to understand anything about the origins of man, you must start by going back to first origins."

"Are you sure?" asked Douglas, after a moment.

"What a question! It stands to reason!"

"Not as much as all that," said Douglas.

"Why?"

"It looks to me," said Douglas, "as if there is some confusion somewhere. Between those shells of yours and an elephant, for instance, or even an ape — good: I can see

38

that the problem does not really change in quality. That you can progress from the one to the other, step by step. But between the ape and man . . . or rather, d'you see, between an ape and an individual — and even, if you like, between the human animal and the individual — there I see a gulf. Something that all your yarns about coils can't bridge."

"The soul, no doubt? Well, well, my little Douglas, are you getting devout?"

"I haven't an ounce of faith, my dear Sybil. You know that. I'm as hardened a skeptic as you are."

"Then what are you talking about?"

"Well, if you like, about the fact that . . . that a word like that had to be invented. The soul. Even if you don't believe in it, you've got to admit . . . that since it had to be invented, and invented for man, you see, to distinguish him from the beast . . . it's just because there is in man, in his way of acting . . . but you've already grasped what I mean, I'm sure."

"No. Explain yourself."

"I mean to say . . . in the motives for human conduct there is . . . something . . . something peculiar, something . . . well, specific, quite unique, that can't be found in other species. Were it only for the fact, for instance, that our behavior varies from one generation to the next. It's changing all the time. Animals never vary in their way of life, even in the course of a thousand years. Whereas between my grandfather's way of looking at life, and so of living it, and my own, there's about as far a cry as from a tortoise to a humming bird."

"So what?"

39

"So nothing. You think you can explain that by the evolution of a jawbone?"

"Well, by the convolutions of the brain, at any rate."

Douglas shook his head with exasperation.

"No, you can't. It's not that at all. That doesn't explain a thing. The convolutions haven't evolved since my grandfather's days. Oh, why on earth is it so hard to express ideas comprehensibly?"

Thereupon a huge black shape coming between the skies and them made them raise their heads. It was Professor Kreps. He was so enormous that if he passed a window indoors, his shadow would plunge the whole room into darkness. His crumpled, unpressed trousers were always too tight, and clung to his thighs in a way that made him look like a pachyderm. His eyes, too, between their puffy lids, would take on the elephant's laughing expression, even when he was angry. He had a walrus mustache on which some remnants of his meals were usually impaled. The most surprising thing about him was his voice, as high and fluting as a young boy's.

"Well, children," he said, "no bed tonight?"

He spoke English correctly, but although he had lived in London since those distant times when Nazism had driven him from Germany, he would still introduce some Teutonic idioms.

"Who would want to!" said Sybil. "The night's too lovely! . . . What about you, anyway?"

"I never sleep, as you know."

This was practically true. He seldom went to bed before two or three in the morning, and even then with a book. Now and then he would break off reading and doze a

40

while without ever turning off the light, until at the first gleam of dawn he would sleep soundly for an hour. Then he would get up, feeling fit and fresh.

That night, while the ship was passing from the Gulf of Aden to the Indian Ocean through the phosphorescent water beneath a sky crowded with stars, was a night so soft and luminous, hardly stirred by a faint, warm breeze, that none of the three left the deck till dawn. Kreps recited in German almost the whole of Hofmannsthal, translating him afterwards into an English that was somewhat cumbrous, but not devoid of poetry. And when he came to the stanza "to be sung in the open air," which begins like this:

> *Die Liebste sprach: "Ich halt dich nicht,*
> *Du hast mir nichts geschworn.*
> *Die Menschen soll man halten nicht.*
> *Zieh Deine Strasse hin, mein Freund ...*

and ends like this:

> *Und wenn mein Mund dir suesser ist,*
> *So komm nur wieder zu mir!"* *

Douglas, with all the simplicity of youth, felt his heart swell with emotion and a bitter happiness.

* My beloved said: "I'm not holding you,
  There's nothing you have sworn me.
  Men should not be kept beholden.
  Go and walk your way, my friend ...
  But if my mouth is sweeter for you,
  Well, then, come back to me!"

41

Chapter 5

SIX HUNDRED MILES THROUGH VIRGIN FOREST.
CONVENIENCE OF ERRORS IN DIRECTION. AN
EIGHTY-MILE DRIFT LEADS THE EXPEDITION
OPPORTUNELY TO THE AUTHOR'S CHOSEN PLACE.
PRIMATES ATTACK THE CAMP WITH STONES. AN
ARGUMENT ON THE HABITAT OF APES. THE
ADVANTAGES OF VIRGIN IGNORANCE OVER SPECIAL-
ISTS' BLINKERS. DOUGLAS TRIUMPHS IMMOD-
ESTLY. A FIND MADE BY KREPS CREATES A
SENSATION.

LA vie est lente, *my dear Frances*, mais l'espérance est
violente.* *[Apollinaire was, next to Verlaine, the French
poet Douglas loved best.] Here we are in Suoguarai. To
think that London is on the other side, that we are standing sole to sole, and that for you I'm walking upside
down! And yet the past weeks are nothing to those it will
still take us to reach the site of the finds, across six or
eight hundred miles of virgin forest. The trail the mighty
Kreps blazed through the mangroves, ferns and lianas
ten months ago (merely by charging like a rhinoceros, I
suppose) must long since have grown over. The whole*

* Life flows idly, but hope springs wildly.

region is, in fact, still practically uncharted. It is one of the last blanks on the face of the map.

We shall be setting out immediately. The whole party landed in fine fettle, and our piles of baggage arrived complete. Some more had been got ready here, and awaited us on our arrival. Shall I confess it? I'm rather excited . . .

Frances smiled. How she wished she could hug him, the darling boy! She couldn't help — "How silly," she told herself — lightly brushing the letter with her lips.

The darling boy was the while battling with the mosquitoes in his tent. He was reeking of ammonia, but the insects did not seem to mind. He was wondering if morning would ever come.

That's how it was every night, and that's how it went on being every night, until at last the expedition reached the forest edge. They had been walking for seventy-six days by compass and guesswork, under a solid roof of foliage which defeated the sextant. But where — according to Kreps's indications — they expected to come up against a chain of low, wooded hills, they found themselves face to face with a bare wall of rock rising to twelve or fifteen hundred feet. The sextant, useful at last under the sky they saw again for the first time in months, showed a drift to east of a few degrees only, but amounting after those long days of marching to an error of nearly a hundred miles. Greame and Father Dillighan were impatient to find a pass through to the hill country as soon as possible. They had a stormy quarrel with Kreps, who, now that they had strayed into those strange cliffs, was eager to stay there at least long enough to study their

43

geology, which, he said, seemed to confirm his theory of volcanic ruptures. Sybil took no part in the squabble. She was content to smile. Douglas followed her lead, feeling — even more than she did — gloriously ready for anything.

Kreps won by sheer bulk and stubbornness. They gave him a week for his explorations. After a brief survey he declared that a depression was sure to be found some miles to the southwest. The caravan got going. They found the depression — or more precisely a "fault" — at the place foreseen. A camp was pitched at the foot of the cliff, near a spring. And Kreps pushed off into the narrow defile, with two Malayans and six Papuans for the work.

On the evening of the fifth day a strange thing happened. The camp was attacked with stones, probably by orangoutangs — it was already too dark to identify them. Nor was it quite clear whence they had come. The fringe of the forest was about half a mile away, and it is well known that apes venture little beyond their woods. Douglas suggested that they might have come down from the cliffs, but he was told with some condescension that as anthropoid apes are tree dwellers, his hypothesis was absurd. Douglas asked whether it was not just as absurd that they had attacked the camp since, to his knowledge, apes, far from provoking man, did their best to avoid him. It was further explained that this was by no means constant. If some wandering Negritos had happened to kill a female or its young, the orangs' grudge could be long-lasting. And it even happens that certain apes, such as the lemurs, attack isolated people with stones.

Two days later Douglas was to triumph. Kreps returned from his expedition. He was delighted. He talked volubly of inverted strata of tuff, loess and lapilli of the Miocene, Pliocene and Pleistocene; the others nodded wisely as if he had been talking of China or Ceylon tea, but to poor Douglas it was all double-Dutch. The only thing he could grasp in the whole rigmarole was that Kreps had discovered, among other things, a sort of amphitheater with a tiled floor, like a bathroom, made of slabs of lava. Above all he heard him add: "The place is lousy with apes."

Douglas had not the grace to refrain from grinning as he looked at the others. A sour glance from Pop and Greame conveyed to him clearly that this was held to be pretty bad form. But Sybil behaved more strangely. She threw her arms round Douglas and kissed him on both cheeks.

"The truth will come to us out of the mouths of babes," she said. "We rely too much on our spectacles."

Greame and Father Dillighan suggested that in an unnoticed depression there might possibly be found some low trees, such as the famous bottle trees. But Kreps shook his head. No more sign of a tree than on the palm of his hand. They were troglodyte apes, living in the holes of the crags. Whereupon Pop changed the subject and asked when they would break camp.

"Not so soon," said Kreps, with a seraphic smile behind his walrus mustache.

"What's that? What d'you mean? Eh?" exclaimed Greame, his ruddy face turning brick-red.

"Oh," said Kreps, "I'm ready enough. I've seen what I wanted. But I doubt whether you and Pop will be in a hurry to leave."

He had squeezed his enormous body into a deck chair

and now sprawled there with blissful unconcern for the shivers of its protesting frame. With a roguish air he dangled a massive leg while watching old Cuthbert over the top of his steel-rimmed glasses. There was a fine "suspense," as film people say.

"You've struck something!" cried Sybil at last, not concealing her impatience. Kreps nodded with a smile.

"Don't keep us on tenterhooks!" she cried. "What is it?"

"A skullcap," said Kreps calmly.

He motioned to one of his Malay boys, who disappeared forthwith into the geologist's tent.

"Where did you find it?" demanded Sybil.

"In lapilli of the Pleistocene. And if it isn't more Hominian than the Sinanthrope's, I'll eat my hat."

"Do translate, for the love of Mike!" Douglas implored Sybil in an undertone, bending towards her.

"Presently," said Sybil, almost sharply. "What makes you say that?" she asked Kreps.

"You'll have a look at the parietal. Anyway, what remains of it," said Kreps.

The Malay came towards them, a box in his hands. Kreps opened it with care. The box was full of sand which must have been very finely sifted, so light it was. Kreps's fat fingers brushed it aside with surprising deftness and skill. He pulled out from it a blanched object, long and rounded, which he placed in Sybil's outstretched palms. Greame and Father Dillighan had drawn closer without a word. They were as pale — that is to say, as little red — as either of them could be. They bent over Sybil's shoulder.

What happened next defies all description.

46

Chapter 6

A BRIEF ELEMENTARY COURSE IN HUMAN
GENETICS FOR THE BENEFIT OF WOMEN — AND
MEN — OF LETTERS. TEN THOUSAND CENTURIES
DROP AWAY BEFORE A THIRTY-YEAR-OLD SKULL.
UNHOPED-FOR SURVIVAL OF FOSSIL APE MAN.
MAN OR APE? DOUGLAS WANTS AN ANSWER BUT
SYBIL AND SCIENTIFIC OBJECTIVITY SEND HIM
PACKING. THE TROPIS' BIRTH AND FORTUNES.

I DID *not imagine, my dear, dear Frances, that I should
be able to send you news so quickly. We are seven
hundred miles from any inhabited locality, or at least
from any civilized one. Before us rises the impassable
range of the Takura Mountains, and behind us the hardly
more penetrable virgin forest. There is no possible link
with the outside world.*

*At least, there wasn't until today. But everything has
been turned upside down by a discovery of Kreps's,
which I will try — if I can — to explain to you — if I can.*

*Our ignorance, dearest Frances, is scandalous. Do you
know (other than by the vaguest hearsay) what are the*

Pithecanthropus *and the* Australopithecus, *the* Sinanthropus, *and the Neanderthal man? Our lack of curiosity about our origins makes me really ashamed. I am absolutely gripped by it now, imagine! And luckily Sybil has angelic patience with me (not always: she sometimes snaps at me as if I were a kid of twelve — that's when I have unwittingly barged into her train of thoughts). Well, this is what you must know: the origins of man and ape — that is practically certain now — go back to one single common stock. This stock "deployed" (that's the technical term), which is to say that under the stress of different environments it branched out in various divergent directions. At the end of those branches or "deployments," you have nowadays all the ape and monkey families on one side, and all the human races on the other. Thus man does not descend from the ape, but apes and man have descended, each on his own side, from the same original stock.*

However, among that welter of branches, there were many forms that prospered for a time, then died out. In deposits of the Pliocene and Pleistocene — sorry! in the geological strata of one or two millions years ago — have been found a quantity of remains of various ape species that have been extinct for thousands of years. They have also found — in Java, China, and the Transvaal — skulls or fragments of skulls of almost human animals that have died out, too. It's those animals that are called Pithecanthropus *(which means ape man), or* Australopithecus *(Southern ape) or* Sinanthropus *(China or Peking man). Their skulls (differing considerably among themselves) are more highly developed than those*

48

of the greatest living apes of today, but less developed than those of the most primitive man. They are halfway.

Among anthropologists, some — like Greame and Sybil — think that these animals are our direct ancestors; the others — like Father Dillighan (perhaps for theological reasons: that's Sybil's idea, anyway) think that they are the end of a separate deployment which became extinct six or eight hundred thousand years ago, perhaps exterminated by the nearest branch of real men, with their greater cruelty and brain power.

I have just written "they think" in the present tense. I ought to have put it in the past. Because for these last few days they've no longer dared to think anything at all . . .

Frances, my darling, I suddenly feel how far away you are. It's not being able to ask you, as I so often used to: "I'm not boring you, am I? I can go on?"

Well, I must just go on without waiting for your answer. Oh please, darling, be patient. I am now so enthralled by all these things! I couldn't bear to think that they make you yawn . . . .

Well, some ten days ago, Kreps discovered, in a volcanic landslide dating back some thousands of centuries, a piece of skull which he brought back. According to him it was a skull somewhere between the Sinanthrope's (one of the fossil apes nearest to man) and Neanderthal man's (the fossil man nearest to the apes.) He thought he was thus bringing grist to the mill of the two Greames, since the existence, long ago, of that equivocal being, still ape and already man, would support their assumption of a single lineage.

49

I wonder, Frances, if you'll react as I did. When I had grasped all this, I felt somehow uneasy, uncomfortable — even deeply disturbed. Sybil thought my question silly. To me, however, that question seemed essential. "Look here," I asked, " 'still an ape and already a man' means what exactly? That it was only an ape, or that it was a man?" "Doug my dear," Sybil told me, "the Greeks for long disputed the earnest question of the precise number of pebbles that make a heap: was it two, three, four, five, or more? Your question is just as nonsensical. All classifications are arbitrary. Nature doesn't classify. It's we who do, because it's convenient. We classify according to premises which, in their turn, are arbitrarily granted. What is it to you, after all, whether this being whose skull I'm holding in my hand is called an ape or a man? He was what he was: the name we give it is immaterial." "You think so?" I said. She shrugged her shoulders. But that was before.

Before we had fully understood what amounts, I believe, Frances, to a major revolution in modern zoology. I'll try — in spite of my impatience to blow the gaff — to tell you events in their proper order.

Well, then, Kreps brought that skullcap back from his trip. Kreps, of course, is a geologist: he knows vastly more about old bones than people like you and me, but paleontology is not, after all, his special field of study. As this skull was buried in an ancient deposit, and completely covered with sediment, he thought it, too, was ancient and fossilized.

So that at first he didn't understand what was happening, any better than I did, when old Greame, after studying the skull for a moment, suddenly went wild with fury.

50

He literally bounded at Kreps, swearing like a trooper. On the face of it, this rage seems quite inexplicable. What could he hold against Kreps, anyway? A bad joke, at worst. Yet now, thinking back to it, the underlying reason for that disproportionate rage seems much clearer to me than it could have been at the time to old Cuthbert himself: his scientific instinct had grasped all that was implied even before his reason did, and he must have felt at once such hopes and — if it was a joke — such disappointment, that his rage acted as a safety valve for his feelings.

Sybil always takes things more calmly. She may also have taken a little longer to grasp what her more experienced husband had seen in a flash. Anyway, the next to understand was Pop. I saw him suddenly bounce off his feet into the air, like a little girl with a skipping rope. He went bouncing like that all round Sybil, who was holding the skull in her hands. So, what with Greame yelling, and Pop skipping, and Sybil slowly turning to marble, I didn't feel too easy in my mind, I assure you!

Kreps at last hoisted his big body out of the deck chair. He brushed Greame aside as one would a fly, went up to Sybil and took the skull from her hands. He next pulled out his penknife and started scraping. And then I heard the finest collection of German oaths you could hope for in a lifetime.

Because that skull, Frances, wasn't fossilized. It was an ape man's skull all right — one of those species that have been extinct for half a million years — but it wasn't a fossil at all! It was, on the contrary, of quite recent date, twenty or thirty years old at most.

You're beginning to understand, I suppose. When Pop

51

*finally managed to pull himself together, he shouted,
"The pebbles!" and we saw him bound through the camp
and pick up the stones which the apes had shied at us two
nights earlier. It's odd, Frances, how quickly the mind
works when it's excited. I knew at once why Pop was
looking for those stones. To see whether they were chipped. You know, like those arrowheads or flint hatchets
that are found in the soil of the Stone Age. And it struck
me as obvious (at least I thought so . . .) that if the apes
who'd thrown them knew how to chip stone, then they
weren't apes, but men.*

The stones were *chipped, Frances. With outstanding
skill and care, even. They are what are apparently called
"hand axes": that is, primitive weapons which these
creatures use to kill their prey more effectively.*

*Mind you, this discovery did not flatly contradict what
had already been suspected. Indeed, around the remains
of the* Sinanthropus *(the fossil ape that lived a million
years ago and was brought to light not far from Peking),
chipped stones and traces of fire had been found, too.
Which started off a great debate. It is proof, said the ones,
that the ape, at that level of intelligence, was already
capable of making fire and manufacturing tools. Not at
all, retorted the others: it is only proof that, contrary to all
belief, men already existed at that time, killed the* Sinanthropus *with those stones and roasted him on that fire.*

We have just had proof that the former were right.

*For it seems beyond doubt, too, that by their zoological
structure the creatures who pelted us with those chipped
pebbles are not men, but apes. Greame, Pop, and Sybil
have already been able to study them pretty closely —*

I'll tell you how presently. I leave you to imagine how excited they are! The fact is — so am I! To have found the ape man, the missing link — and to have found it alive! We've since unearthed hundreds of skulls like the one Kreps brought back — for it turns out that these strange apes bury their dead. We have discovered a real necropolis — rough and primitive of course, but its funerary character is certain. All the same, they are apes. Of course, I don't know much about it, but you have but to look at them. They have very long arms, and though they generally hold themselves erect, they do at times, when running fast, use the back of their fingers as a support, the way chimpanzees do. Their body is covered with hair, but I must say that there is something disturbing about it, especially with the females. They are slighter than the males, their arms are not so long, and they have real hips and very feminine breasts. Their fur is very short and soft, a little like that of moles. All this gives them a graceful, delicate appearance — rather appealing, almost sensual; but the face is terrible.

For it is bare, like that of human beings. But almost as flattened as that of the apes. The forehead is low and receding, the browline jutting, the nose almost nonexistent, the mouth protruding like that of Negroes, but lipless like gorillas, with mighty teeth and fang-like canines. The males have a sort of daisy chain that makes them look like old sailors of earlier days. The females have a silken fringe that falls over their eyes. They are very gentle and only ask to be tamed. The males are of uncertain temper, mostly peaceful and quiet, but subject to sudden outbursts of rage that call for careful handling.

53

As you see, I speak of them as apes — male and female. But it's very tempting to speak of them as human beings, since they chip stones, make fire, bury their dead, and even communicate with each other by means of a sort of language — a small number of articulate cries which Pop estimates at about a hundred.

Well, that's as far as we've got. For the time being the question of what to call them remains open. To tell you the truth, I'm afraid I'm the only one who really worries about it. I told you Sybil's reply to me: "What does it matter?" At first sight it seems, indeed, that she is right. Greame, Kreps, and she have provisionally settled the question by referring to them familiarly as tropis *(no doubt because it's a contraction of* anth opus *and* pithecus). *Oddly enough, Pop seems to dislike using this word, though it's really rather a nice one. He always refers to them in a roundabout way, obviously not daring to say either "apes" or "men" or "tropis." This indecision seems to weigh on him as it does on me, or even more. Yes, come to think of it, even more. For I have finally adopted "tropis" like the others. It's easier. But on the understanding, in my own mind, that it is only "for the time being." It will jolly well have to be decided one day whether they are apes or men . . .*

Chapter 7

FATHER DILLIGHAN'S DISTRESS AND INDECISION. .
HAVE THE TROPIS GOT A SOUL? THE APE MEN'S
CUSTOMS AND LANGUAGE. DO THEY ALREADY LIVE
IN ORIGINAL SIN, OR STILL IN BEAST-LIKE IN-
NOCENCE? TO CHRISTEN OR NOT TO CHRISTEN.
STUDY, EXPERIMENT, AND OBSERVATION SERVE,
AS USUAL, ONLY TO ENHANCE UNCERTAINTY.

My *dearest Douglas, how wonderful to be able to write
to you, in my turn. You didn't tell me — you had too
much to say! — by what miracle your letters reach me
from the depths of your wilderness, nor how mine will
cross your mountains or your virgin forest. But you would
not have begged me so eagerly for an answer, if my letter
were to languish poste restante in Suoguarai.*

*What an adventure, Douglas, what a discovery! Your
fever of excitement has proved thoroughly catching. I
promptly went and bought up everything that has come
out in England on the great apes and fossil man. I'm up
to my ears in it already. The technical jargon is a bit
formidable at first, but I'm beginning to hack my way*

55

through that particular jungle. Is it because I love you, Douglas, but I react just as you do: the existence of your tropis fills me with a real malaise. I don't yet know why, exactly. Maybe it's a survival of the old beliefs I was brought up in: at times I catch myself thinking that we've absolutely got to know whether your tropis have a soul or not. The fact is, even the most skeptical among us cannot altogether reject the idea that man alone was given a divine spark. Yes, isn't that the source of our uneasiness? If man has slowly descended from the beast, at what moment did he receive that spark? Before being a tropi, or after? Or during? Doesn't the whole question, Douglas, boil down to this: have your tropis got a soul? What does Father Dillighan think about it? . . .*

Poor Father Dillighan was suffering torments precisely because he did not know what to think. During the first days the scientific fever alone had held him in its grip. He had worked with the same fervor and enthusiasm as the others. Then they saw him growing anxious and distracted, and sinking into fitful silence and sullenness. While he was listening to Sybil and Douglas arguing about the nature, human or otherwise, of the tropis, his red, horsey face would grow pale, his heavy lips would move with soundless mutterings, and it would even happen that he let his pipe go out. One day, when Sybil had cut Douglas short with an exasperated, "Oh, leave me alone, for Pete's sake!" Pop had taken the young man by the arm and confided in his ear:

"You're jolly well right. At moments like this, science makes me sick."

56

He held Douglas's arm tightly, as if he were clinging to it.

"Do you know what I think?" he asked in a voice that had suddenly turned husky. "We all deserve to be damned!"

He jerked his head round towards the young man as if to catch his reaction. Douglas certainly did not hide his surprise.

"Who all? All men of science?"

"No, no," Pop quickly corrected himself, shaking his silver mop of hair. "All we men of faith and devotion."

He dropped his companion's arm and walked on with bent head. "We lack imagination to a quite damnable degree," he said. "An adventure like this opens really terrifying perspectives."

He raised his head, and Douglas saw real anguish brimming in his eyes.

"Not quite twenty centuries have passed since Jesus came, and five thousand since men first started to exist," Pop went on, "five thousand centuries during which they lived in ignorance and sin. Do you realize what that means? And our charity is so feeble that we never even think of it. Why, the mere thought of them should make us sweat with love and anguish. But we are quite content to worry about the salvation of a handful of the living."

"You think that God has damned them? I thought that doctrine held, since they sinned in innocence . . ."

"I know . . . I know . . . perhaps they are in limbo . . . It's a way of comforting ourselves . . . But do you think it is less dreadful to wander for all eternity in the awful emptiness of limbo, than to burn in hell? Our ingrained

57

sense of justice revolts at the thought . . . but God's justice is not ours. We do not know its purpose.

"Do you imagine," he muttered, "that all this leaves me with a quiet mind? What happiness can be mine at the right hand of God, if my sins are absolved, knowing that less fortunate souls in their millions are suffering fire and brimstone? I should feel like a Nazi celebrating a family Christmas and rejoicing over the concentration camps."

He raised his arm towards the compound where the captured tropis had been parked.

"What should one do about them?" he said, and it was as if he had shouted softly. "Must they be abandoned in their innocence? But *are* they in a state of innocence at all? If they are human, they are sinners: and they have received no sacrament! Must they be left to live and die without baptism, with all that awaits them hereafter, or else . . ."

"What are you thinking of, Pop? cried Douglas in amazement. "Not of baptizing them, surely?"

"I don't know," muttered Pop, "I really don't know, and it's destroying me utterly."

∽

It might be as well, perhaps, to fill in some gaps Douglas left in his account. He had too much to tell to think of everything. It was only little by little that Frances learned of the exploits of the Greame expedition since Kreps's sensational discovery.

As soon as the first excitement had passed, the scientific

58

spirit resumed its sway; that is to say, the spirit of observation, which is, again, the practical spirit — how best to use this incredible stroke of luck, extract the most from it for science?

To begin with, the camp moved to the famous amphitheater "tiled with lava, like a bathroom," so as to be nearer the tropis. The tiled floor was soon found to be artificial: they saw that each slab covered a natural pocket, large or small — the lava at the spot was pitted with holes like a Gruyère cheese — and that most of the holes were filled with bones.

It did not take Pop and the Greames long to assemble the fragments. This produced perfectly constituted skeletons of four-handed creatures which, on the whole, though, came closer to the human skeleton than any of the fossil apes found hitherto, including even Peking man. Yet they were less highly developed than that fossil creature which — despite its disproportionate limbs and the forward set of its narrow skull on the slanting backbone — is no longer called an ape, but Neanderthal *man*, because of the various hand-fashioned tools that were found near him.

For more than a week they did not catch sight of any live tropis. No doubt the invasion had frightened them away. Their absence made it possible to explore their deserted caves. In all of them could be found traces of fire, litters of leaves, and an incredible number of hand axes. The walls, however, were bare: no drawings or marks of any sort.

Numerous remains showed that the tropis, unlike the great apes who live on roots and fruit and occasional

59

insects, were to some extent carnivorous. Their fires, it was clear, had served, not to cook meat, but to smoke it crudely. Some abandoned morsels of tapir and porcupine, thus smoked, were found hidden under pieces of rock, the tropis having probably been unable to take them along in their flight.

"Creatures able to do all that must surely be human!" Douglas had cried.

"Don't get excited," said Sybil. "You haven't seen beavers build their dams, divert the course of a stream, turn reeking swamps into cities far healthier than Bruges or Venice? Do you know that ants preserve fungi, breed livestock? And that they too have burial places for their dead? Below a certain level of industry, you can't tell at first sight whether you're up against instinct or intelligence. You certainly can't base a zoological classification on those things, not a really scientific one. And anyway, even if a horse learned to play the piano like Brailowsky, it wouldn't be a man for all that. It would still be a horse."

"But you wouldn't send it to the knackers," said Douglas.

"You mix up everything," said Sybil. "That's not the question!"

"Perhaps not for your fossil apes of a million years ago — and even there Pop would have a word to say about it. But these tropis are alive!"

"So what?"

"Oh hell!" shouted Douglas, beside himself. "I'm beginning to wonder whether you yourself are a human being, or a walking table of logarithms!"

60

He saw Pop encourage him with a smile, and that restored his self-control.

In the meantime, Greame had set going the small radio transmitter which had been intended for use only in an emergency. The message he sent to Suoguarai was immediately relayed to Sydney and Borneo. It was later learned that the Natural History Museum of Borneo had merely — if one may say so — shrugged its shoulders. But Sydney got excited. A wealthy amateur anthropologist lent a helicopter and, soon after, another. Two weeks later the camp had grown by six new tents, a doctor, a surgeon-anatomist, two film operators, a biochemist with a portable laboratory, two workmen with three tons of wire netting and steel props, and a staggering quantity of canned ham.

For it had been found that the tropis were extremely fond of ham. They had, in fact, returned to their caves after a few days, at first timidly, then with joyous haste as the firstcomers found the ham which the Greames had scattered there at random. Fires were lighted everywhere to smoke it — an odd procedure since it was to be eaten at once. And the cliffs resounded once more with what Kreps called their chatter, and Pop their language.

"Language!" mocked Kreps. "Because they say 'outch' when they hurt themselves, and 'yip-hi-dee' when they're happy?"

"They say neither 'outch' nor 'yip-hi-dee,'" replied Pop earnestly. "You can distinguish precise sounds, I assure you. They aren't like ours, that's why you don't recognize them. But they are perfectly distinguishable

61

once you've isolated them. I'm already beginning to understand them."

Kreps proved less sarcastic when, a few days later, Pop tried an experiment, and was successful. He gave two short cries, and a strange silence immediately fell upon the cliff; another cry, and hundreds of tropis appeared together at the mouth of their caves; two or three more cries, but after a pause, as if of expectancy or hesitation, the tropis disappeared, chattering.

"What did you say to them?" cried Kreps.

"Nothing," said Pop. "The first cries I gave were alerts; then one that you might call "for unusual circumstances"; I meant the last two to intrigue them even more: it's what they shout to indicate the flight of wild birds. Anyway, that's what I'd thought, and I hoped that they would at least raise their heads. But I must have misunderstood, or else mispronounced them."

"Be that as it may," said Douglas. "Professor Kreps is right: they are cries, not a language."

"What do you call language?" asked Pop. "If a grammar and syntax are required to deserve that name, many a primitive tribe cannot be said to talk. The Veddas of Ceylon have only a hundred words or so which they content themselves with reeling off one after another. I say that there is language when articulate sounds denote objects or facts, sensations or feelings, which differ according to the position and the choice of sound."

"Why, then, according to you, the birds talk?"

"If you like — but their cries are too poor indistinct modulations really to qualify as a language."

"Whereas the cries of the tropis are sufficiently modulated? We're getting back to the story of the heap of pebbles," sighed Douglas. "How many words or distinct sounds are needed to deserve the name of language?"

"Ay, there's the rub!" admitted Pop.

∾

Thus every time poor Douglas thought he held a guideline, he would see it slip again through his fingers, or at least lead him to no certainty. His only comfort — if it was one — was to know Pop even more distressed than himself.

"Look here, Pop," he said, "there's no sense in your worrying: even if the tropis are human, how can you christen them without their consent?"

"If you had to wait for people's consent before christening them," sighed Pop, "no newborn babies would ever be baptized."

"That's true! Why, indeed, Pop, do you christen them?"

"Saint Augustine is quite definite in his reply to Pelagus," said Pop. "The soul of the child, as it comes into the world, is laden with all the weight of original sin. 'The Catholic faith teaches,' he says, 'that all men are born so guilty that even children are sure to be damned if they die without having been regenerated in Jesus.' As a Benedictine I cannot doubt the word of him to whom we owe all that is best in our Order. So if the tropis are human, even though they sin in innocence, they are guilty. Only baptism can wash them of original sin until such time as, having come to reason, they understand what they are doing and become responsible for their own salvation. Until then, all those who die without bap-

63

tism are promised at least the eternal silence of limbo, if not the flames of hell. How could I bear the thought that, by my abstention, I may be the cause of such unspeakable misery for them?"

"Well, then," said Douglas, "christen them! What's the risk?"

"But if they are beasts, Douglas, you couldn't think of giving them the sacrament! It would be an ungodly act! Remember," he added, smilingly now, "remember the poor old blundering Saint Mael, whose eyesight was so poor that he mistook a tribe of penguins for a lot of gentle savages, and proceeded to baptize them forthwith. Which, the chronicler tells us, put heaven in a great predicament: how were the souls of penguins to be received at the right hand of God? A council of archangels decided that the only way out of the quandary was to change them into men. Which was done. Whereupon all those poor penguins ceased sinning in innocence, and were well and truly damned."

"Then don't baptize them!"

"But if they are human, Douglas!"

These vacillations of Father Dillighan's managed to make Sybil cry with laughter. She got him to explain to her the Encyclical *Humani generis*, which defines the zoological boundary line that the Church deems proper to draw between the beast and man. "But that's just it: those confounded tropis keep straddling that boundary!" cried Pop. "Like Chaplin at the Mexico-Texas frontier, at the end of *The Pilgrim*. One foot on each side," he groaned.

"Come, come, Pop," Sybil would say. "A little patience.

The house isn't on fire. All those good tropis can manage without baptism for a few months longer!"

"But those who'll die meanwhile?"

They did indeed seem to die with the greatest of ease, and at all ages — which offset to some extent their remarkable fertility. Hardly a day passed without some tropis being seen to drag a body from its cave. But no member of the expedition had yet managed to observe one of the funerals. Whether it was the camp's proximity to their burial place that had caused the tropis to abandon it, or whether they had done so at an earlier date, the fact was that they would clamber up the cliffs with a monkey's nimbleness and disappear into the lava-covered valleys, bearing their macabre loads.

We afterwards had no trouble in finding the bodies [wrote Douglas to Frances]. And it looks as if the survivors never noticed our depredations: four nights running we removed the bodies from the same lava pocket into which they had just put them. The fifth time we left the slab in its place: only then did they pass on to the next hole.

I've been present while Theo and Willy (the doc and the surgeon) dissected some of the bodies. Always the same result: certain organs are almost human, others still have the characteristics of the great apes. Impossible to decide from the evidence. The brain in particular is disturbing. It apparently presents most of the convolutions of our brain. But the grooves are shallower, the ridges less pronounced. There is nothing, though, according to Willy, that would preclude the training of their intel-

65

ligence. You could even go pretty far with it, he thinks.

Since my last letter, we have managed to capture some tropis — male, female and children, some thirty in all. Capture is not the right word. We have lured and seduced them. Lured them with ham, seduced them with the radio. Naturally these are the least timid ones. And the biggest spongers. So much so that they've ended by dogging our footsteps and never leaving the camp. We have arranged a compound for them nearby — out of sight of their fellows. They are happy there and make no attempt to leave. Every day, some fresh tropis come prowling around the camp begging, and join the others. In spite of the wire netting all around them, I don't think they've realized that they are in captivity.

We have given them no end of intelligence tests. Since you've read The Great Apes, *you know how this is done. And that the results are staggering: for instance, while the chimpanzee is cleverer than the orangoutang and much quicker at solving problems requiring ingenuity (such as getting hold of a fruit that is out of reach, opening a lock, and so on), the orang has shown a capacity for reflection quite unexpected in an animal — in using, for example, an iron rod to bend apart the bars of its cage, thus inventing the lever.*

Our tropis seem scarcely more advanced than they. Their hands are nimbler — rather like those of the Pygmies, with long autonomous fingers (they often point to a distant object with their forefinger, in a very human gesture). But what they can do with their hands is limited. They make fire by rubbing two chipped flints over lichen. We have lighted paper with matches in front of them. At first they were simply scared. Then their curiosity got the better of them. They watched us for quite a while, tried to imitate us, but took a considerable time to establish the link between cause and effect. At last the most intelligent one among them succeeded in grasping the role of the match. But he has not made any headway since in choosing the end to strike. If he does strike the right end, it is by accident.

On the other hand, Pop has really succeeded in teaching them to say five or six words in English — the English of a child of three. The first word they could say was "ham," then "zik" to clamor for the radio, which they are crazy about. But apparently this doesn't yet prove anything. Years ago, Pop tells me, someone named Furness obtained results of the same order with an orang-outang. Pop says we have to see whether the tropis later link these words in ideas.

Pop has even managed to bring one of them to the point of recognizing the letter H by making him want pieces of ham on which that letter was drawn. The tropi can pick it out from among the others, say "ham" when he sees it, and now, even trace the letter with a pencil. But he dislikes all rewardless effort and does not know what to do with a pencil when he is no longer hungry. He showed no interest at all in the drawings that Pop kept making in front of him, nor, generally speaking, in any pictures or photographs. It is clear that he does not "see" them.

Everything in this field would seem to link the tropis to the ape rather than to man. But many other facts point in the opposite direction. Their face, though still so near that of the orangoutang, is much more expressive. First of all, they can laugh: and if laughter is the mark of man, they are as human as you and I. I wouldn't go so far as to say that they have a sense of humor! But any clowning that would make a child of two laugh makes them laugh, too.

They are particularly remarkable to watch as they work their hand axes. If their bodies were not covered with that short tawny fur, if their bent posture were not rather like a gorilla's, and, finally, if they had not four hands, those too-short legs and too-long arms, that receding forehead and those fangs, you'd think you were watching some primitive craftsman or sculptor at his work. They strike the stone with incredible precision, first chipping off large flakes, then ever smaller ones, and finally tapping it lightly and delicately until it at last assumes that familiar shape of an egg with cutting edges, which almost all of us, in the camp, would be quite unable to fashion.

The strange thing is that all day long they go on making heaps of these hand axes, although they have no more opportunities for using them — those in the compound, I mean. Even the very young ones try their hand at it. They do it clumsily, hit their fingers at times — and all the others laugh.

One day Pop had the idea of chipping a stone in front of them with a real hammer and chisel. They did not know how to use the chisel, but were soon quarreling noisily about the hammer: they had realized that the stones could be shaped more quickly. Thus they are capable of improving their tools, but not of grasping that these have ceased to serve a purpose. Like those doe rab-

bits who, in spite of having a ready-made nest put beside them when they're about to have their litter, go on tearing out their fur and no longer know what to do with it.

You see, Frances, that we are making very little headway. Or rather, I'm not, for I am alone — with Pop — in plaguing myself to know whether or not they belong to the human species.

These last days I have again had almost a real quarrel with Sybil. She said to me:

"This question is not only fatuous, it would actually hamper our work. Our job is to make objective observations. If we set out to 'prove' anything, no matter what, we're done for. Your mind's been warped by journalism, Douglas! You think in headlines: 'Are the tropis human?' But science isn't interested in such catchpenny phrases. So be a good boy and run along, and stop bothering me with all this nonsense, once and for all!"

"All right," I answered. "But suppose I feel like hunting tomorrow and use them as game? Would you let me?"

"Don't be an ass, Douglas. You've no more right to kill them than chimpanzees or the duck-billed platypus. There's a law protecting any species threatened with extinction."

"I wouldn't be very proud of that answer, if I were you. But let me put it differently: if we were starving, and had no food or other game within reach, would you eat a tropi and think no more of it?"

She got up, protesting: "Douglas, you're beastly!" and walked straight out of the tent. But she hadn't given me an answer. . . .

69

Chapter 8

MAY THE TROPIS SERVE AS ROASTS FOR CHRISTIAN
CREATURES? THE PAPUAN PORTERS SOLVE THE
QUESTION. FATHER DILLIGHAN'S INCREASED
DISTRESS AND THE CAMP'S CONSTERNATION. THE
TROPIS GO VISITING. THEIR FRIENDSHIP FOR
DOUGLAS AND HIS COMPANIONS. SCIENTIFIC OB-
JECTIVITY IS ROUTED FOR THE FIRST TIME. THE
TAKURA DEVELOPMENT CORPORATION. AUSTRAL-
IAN WOOL INTERESTS AND BRITISH COMPETITION.
INDUSTRIAL PLANS BASED ON FREE MAN POWER.
WILL THE TROPIS BE SOLD AS BEASTS OF BURDEN?
SCIENTIFIC OBJECTIVITY IS ROUTED FOR THE
SECOND TIME. THE EGG OF COLUMBUS. A DELICATE
PROPOSITION. FATHER DILLIGHAN'S INDIGNATION.

THAT was, however, the very way in which the question
did arise one day. Or rather, one night, when the camp
of the Papuan carriers was bright with the glare of unac-
customed bonfires. "What can they be up to?" Kreps
wondered. Douglas saw Father Dillighan rise and silently
delve into the darkness, towards the firelit camp, where

70

what looked like wildly moving, dancing shadows showed up dark against the flames.

"The shepherd is uneasy about his flock," mocked Sybil. "Their faith is not yet built on a rock."

Pop was often teased about his conversions among the Papuans. All his efforts, for instance, to make them give up tattooing had been utterly unsuccessful. His converts would merely add to their more usual motifs an occasional cross or crown of thorns. At such times Pop would fly into a thundering rage under which his neophytes' backs buckled with terror.

Douglas and his friends cocked their ears, waiting for the expected outburst. But they heard nothing.

And when the Benedictine came back, they saw that he looked pale and drawn.

"Well," said Kreps, "what is it they're doing? Celebrating Vishnu, or the moon, or what?"

Pop raised bewildered eyes to him. Then he shook his white curls and slowly imitated a spit being turned. At last he said:

"They're roasting them."

"Roasting whom? Vishnu and the moon?"

"No. The tropis."

Two months earlier, this "tropophagy" would probably not have seemed of much consequence to anyone in the camp — save Pop and Douglas. They would have scolded the Papuans, threatened them with punishment in case of relapse. Perhaps they would even have laughed up their sleeve, like the parents of mischievous children.

But the feelings of them all — even Kreps's and Sybil's — had meanwhile undergone a marked change. They had

71

gradually passed from experimental detachment to a real budding affection.

Affection and, in certain cases, even genuine respect. Not of course for the tame, domesticated tropis in the compound, whom they had grown fond of as you are fond of faithful pets whose appealing ways amuse you. But they soon realized that the reserve of the others, of those who fiercely clung to their cliffs, was due not so much to fear or distrust, as to a more meticulous regard for their independence.

While the former had at once approached the camp in small chattering bands, fickle, frivolous, begging for ham — that ham for the love of which they had eventually renounced their freedom — these others, on the contrary, let several weeks go by before honoring the camp with a first visit.

And then, one fine morning, an old tropi was seen coming along, all by himself. He approached the camp without haste, but without fear; and, as if it were the most normal thing in the world, he strolled slowly among the tents with the lounging, slightly aloof manner of a visitor to a World Fair. At first the people in the camp let him be, as if they hardly noticed him. So he stopped here and there to gaze at things and people, as naturally as a London window-shopper. He displayed interest in the washing fluttering in the wind, seemed startled at the sight of the helicopter in its shed, intrigued by the running motor of the electric generator, fascinated by the mechanics shaving themselves, their faces covered with lather.

At last Father Dillighan came slowly towards him and,

72

when some ten steps away, emitted a short, liquid sound. The old tropi did not start, he just looked Pop up and down, but said nothing. Pop smiled without moving and again murmured the same mellow sound, to which there still came no reply. He only saw the tropi's left hand take the hand ax that he must have all along held concealed in his right hand, and pass it slowly over his hairy chest in a gentle, peaceful gesture.

Nothing more happened that day. As the tropi was leaving, Douglas tried to offer him half a ham, only to be snubbed by a display of ostentatious indifference. He did not insist, and the old tropi ambled back to his cliff with noble calm.

The next day they came, ten or twelve strong. Was the old tropi of the previous day with them? They were too much alike, or at least their hosts were still too unpracticed in telling them apart, for it to be certain. But this much was sure: they were all of them old tropis.

They, in turn, visited the camp with the same loitering interest, like a small party of retired parish clerks up from the country on a sightseeing tour. When any one of them lagged behind, he would fall into a run to catch up with the others, helping himself with his overlong arms, like an ape. It was noticed that they were not all equally fascinated by the same things. The foam-covered faces of the men shaving themselves hardly retained their attention. They all felt drawn to the motor of the electric generator, but the intensity of their interest varied with the individual. One of them even displayed an imperturbable indifference to all that caught his friends' fancy. He would turn back to them with the bored patience of a father trying to drag his small son past a row of toyshop windows.

Greame and Pop, the *doyens* of the camp, were squatting cross-legged between two tents, waiting for them. On the ground they had spread a dozen smoked hams. The old tropis stopped, surprised. Pop produced the brief, liquid sound he had used the day before. There was a vague murmur among the tropis, but at first they did not budge. The two men got up; Pop addressed the tropis with some more mellow sounds, then Greame and he withdrew into the tent. A hasty chatter ran through the band of tropis when they saw they were being left alone. They then proceeded to accept the hams and, all together, made for the cliffs, but this time at a less phlegmatic pace than the previous day's caller.

Thereafter, the visits had grown in frequency. But they were never in the nature of scrounging expeditions. On the contrary, if you had had to name their particular quality, you would have called them "friendly." Yes, it was an impulse of curiosity and goodwill that was clearly driving the tropis, in ever greater numbers, to pay these visits. The less aged ones even showed, in their investigations, the eagerness of little boys being shown round a locomotive works. Gradually they came to enjoy taking part in the camp activities, at least in those that they could imitate without effort. It was noticeable that the females were never brought along.

None of the tropis, however, would stay in the camp for more than a few hours; none passed the night there. A ticklish experiment was tried: the compound was left open. But most of the captives did not go beyond the gates.

74

Those who did, returned to sleep there. "We've scooped all the flunkies!" said Kreps.

One morning, Kreps, Douglas, and Dr. Williams (Willy to his friends) decided to pay a return visit to the cliffs. They were shown the same courtesy that they themselves had extended in the early days: that is to say, they were left alone to walk about, without anyone's apparently paying the slightest heed to them. A few weeks later, the coming and going between cliff and camp had become a ceaseless flow.

Kreps and his companions could thus observe, with growing friendship and respect, that the life of the cliffs was that of a peaceful community, a more than perfect democracy: no chief, nothing even suggesting a council of elders. The younger ones merely imitated or followed their elders in their methods of hunting, their caution or boldness in the face of a collective threat. (The camp, it will be remembered, had been attacked with stones on its first appearance near the cliffs: this was never followed by anything more than a peaceful vigilance.)

There even developed, with time, real individual friendships — not, this time, the submissive attachment of a dog for his master, but the more dignified affection that springs up between equals. Silent friendships, for the simple pleasure of being together: Douglas had three friends of this sort who scarcely left him. One of them had a passion for opening cans of food (though he never touched anything unless expressly invited to do so), the other two for rinsing bottles which they liked to make as shiny as crystal.

Douglas had tried to give them names (they used none

75

among themselves), and to accustom them to respond, but without success. His efforts to teach them his own name proved just as unavailing. It appeared, in general, that any idea of differentiation, of individuality, was completely alien to them.

What seemed odd at first was that the captive tropis *had* eventually learned to answer to the names they had been given. But Pop pointed out, no doubt quite rightly, that the name had for them become associated with the idea of food, and that it probably was with them, as with dogs, a case of conditioned reflexes.

Pop drew attention to another point: when a tropi designated himself he made a sort of inner murmur, an *mmm* which seemed embedded in the depths of his lungs. When, on the contrary, he wished to indicate someone else, he would eject between his teeth a very hard sound, a *ttt*, which he spat violently outwards. Pop wondered whether those two sounds (the one inward, the other outward) might not be at the origin of the words *me* and *thou*, which, in almost all the languages in the world, start with an *m* or with a *t* or *d* respectively.

He also claimed to have real conversations with an old crony, in tropi language — if one accepts this term for a monosyllabic exchange of information to the effect that it is midday or nightfall, hot, cooler, or cold . . . . Their most elaborate talk had turned upon the statement that fire hurts. Pop could not bring his friend further than that. Nor, to be quite just, could the tropi his friend Pop; the latter's gift for languages broke down before many a sonority that proved too elusive.

Sybil was the only one to have no friends among the

cliff dwellers. Not that she had no wish to, or was unsuccessful. But certain too visible signs showed that it was wiser for her not to mingle with the male tropis more than was necessary.

And lastly, the immediate hostility that had sprung up between tropis and Papuans had not passed without notice. Many a time a brawl could only just be averted. The peaceful temper of the tropis suddenly gave way to that of a mastiff encountering another in the street: snarls, hair a-bristle, fangs bared. The Papuans remained silent, but a sudden glint of cruelty oozed from their eyes and from every pore.

Nevertheless, no one foresaw that they would one day indulge in this clandestine tropi-beanfeast. It caused, throughout the camp, a boundless consternation, an explosion of anger mingled with real grief. It took all Father Dillighan's prestige and persuasiveness to prevent too drastic reprisals. Yet no one was more deeply affected by the incident than he, since most of the Papuans were converts to the Christian faith. "But what can we reproach them with?" he asked. "Have they eaten animals, or men? We don't know ourselves; how then can we ask them to know more about it than we do?"

They all listened — unlaughingly, feeling guilty themselves — to Pop pathetically debating whether or not he ought to confess the Papuans for mortal sin. But the latter could easily feign surprise: why weren't they to eat those animals? On what grounds could he exact penitence from them — and how could he absolve them without it? To demand contrition from them for the sin of gluttony would be a sorry piece of cant!

77

Douglas had at least one satisfaction: to see that Sybil dared not look him in the face. But whatever pay-back that was for their recent quarrel, it was soon forgotten. For a last warning, infinitely graver than that of the tropi-eating Papuans, was to prove Douglas and Pop so glaringly right that there was not a single member of the camp, not even Sybil, not even Kreps, who did not wish as much as they to settle definitely that famous question: are the tropis human?

∽

Day after day, the cameramen had been "shooting" the tropis, those of the cliffs whenever they could, but more often the captive ones, especially during tests. This film material was to serve two different purposes: one purely spectacular, for release to the general public, the other scientific, for documentary records and research.

The helicopters going for fresh supplies would fly the reels back to Sydney, to be developed in the laboratory of the Australian firm that had commissioned the cameramen. What exactly happened there? Everything would suggest that among the directors and their guests, before whom these rushes were privately shown, there must have been a certain Vancruysen, one of those big-business sharks always on the lookout for new rackets.

It must be admitted that the last tests to which the domestic tropis had been submitted were extremely suggestive. These were no longer intelligence tests designed to measure their capacity for observation and reflection (which, as has been seen, proved hardly superior to that of the great apes), but performance tests, designed to

78

measure their capacity for learning and carrying out certain actions, operations, or set tasks. It is well known that any chimpanzee can learn very quickly to dress, tie his shoelaces, eat or serve at table, smoke a cigar, or ride on horseback or a bicycle. In colonial households chimpanzees are often seen performing domestic chores, just like servants. The tropis soon progressed beyond the stage of such simple actions. Guided by the two mechanics, they learned with amazing speed to handle the metal frames, distinguish between them, select them, and soon even to assemble them; they could not be taught to use a hand drill effectively, but they visibly enjoyed screwing nuts and bolts. They proved patient in their work, rather in the manner of elephants, provided they were now and then encouraged, patted on the back, and also rewarded with bits of ham. Their muscular strength, moreover, seemed practically inexhaustible.

That they should accordingly strike Vancruysen as a marvelously cheap and docile form of man power will surprise no one. The details, after all, matter little. The fact is that Vancruysen remembered the existence of an old, half-dormant company, the Takura Development Corporation, founded some ten or twelve years previously for the purpose of prospecting the subsoil of that unexplored range. There had been hopes of finding a layer of naphtha at the northern tip. That layer did indeed exist, but was exhausted within two years. Instead, there were found, farther west, some hundred acres of rubber trees, whose exploitation enabled the company to eke out a living. They also let hunts in the plain to private parties. All this, no doubt, gave Vancruysen the idea that the

79

concession granted to the Development Corporation must have comprised the exclusive right to exploit the fauna and flora of the entire Takura region. To check the matter was easy; and also to discover that, in consequence, the Corporation found itself owning all the tropis on the cliffs as well as any that might yet be discovered in other valleys of the range.

Vancruysen himself controlled in Sydney one of the largest processing companies for the by-products of wool. He got it to buy up cheaply the bulk of the shares in the Takura Corporation. Once these were in his pocket, he went to see a man named Granett, who had one foot in the government and one in wool production.

It is a known fact that immigration to Australia is rigidly restricted and controlled. The living standard, on the other hand, is high. It follows that man power is scarce and costly. That is why the enormous annual yield of wool from the huge flocks in the plains cannot be manufactured on the spot: cloth made under these conditions would not be able to compete against English prices. The wool is therefore shipped raw to England, and processed and woven there.

"Did you see those films about the tropis?" Vancruysen asked Granett.

"No," replied the other. "What are they?"

"Come along," said Vancruysen.

He took him to see the film.

"What d'you think of them?" he asked afterwards.

"Well . . ." began Granett . . .

"Imagine them in a spinning mill," said Vancruysen. "Three tropis to one operative . . ."

Granett stared at him, and remained open-jawed.

"I've gone into the figures," said Vancruysen. "Thirty or forty thousand tropis, given the right training, and working under skilled foremen, could handle two thirds of the Continent's output. Cost: their food and a little care. We'd beat the English spinners by six lengths."

"God Almighty!" muttered Granett. "We'd sweep them right out of the American market!"

"Without taking our coats off!" said Vancruysen, with a laugh. "The number of tropis in the Takura is reckoned, I think, at two or three thousand. The animal seems adult at ten. In four or five years a thousand females could produce the necessary livestock. In twelve or fifteen at the outside, the mills would be going full blast."

"What do you need?" asked Granett.

"Capital, of course," said Vancruysen. "And government support."

"As to capital, the sheep breeders will give you that."

"Don't want theirs," said Vancruysen. "I want the banks'."

"Why?"

Vancruysen grinned, and asked:

"You didn't look at them very closely, did you?"

"At whom? The sheep breeders?"

"No, me lad. The tropis. They look a bit too much like real people."

Granett shrugged his shoulders, smiling.

"That's all very well," said Vancruysen. "But d'you think the English'll just sit and smile?"

"You think . . ."

"Sure. They'll throw a spanner in the works; raise the

81

issue of our moral right to exploit those half-animals, and the whole shoot. It's on the cards."

"I still don't see why the banks . . ."

"They must be in it," said Vancruysen, "up to their necks. If there's a court action later, and the judge has to choose between the moral rights of the tropis and the foundering of Australian banking credit, it's Hobson's choice. Right?"

"It's a cinch. How are you going to set about it?"

"It depends on you government people. You'll have to subsidize the immediate building of the mills, with all modern equipment. Never mind the amount of the subsidy: that's just to get the banks to follow on with the necessary millions. . . . Get the idea? People would be crazy if they afterwards let all that money go down the drain. Once the tropis are in, they'll stay in. Anyway, we won't wait for them to get here before building them a model camp, with dormitories, infirmary, canteen, doctors, zoologists, the whole caboodle. . . . Not forgetting a vast experimental clinic. Because we'll have to develop the tropis' working capacity, and hurry up the breeding-pace of the females. That can be brought about by selection, I think. You're a bit of a breeder. That should be up your alley."

"Yes, indeed," said Granett, "and moreover," he suggested, "you ought to think about gelding the males. Your film shows that their main failing is their uncertain temper. I'm sure it will be with them as with all domestic animals: gelding will make them more tractable without reducing their output."

"That's a brilliant idea!" said Vancruysen.

☙

Granett set to work with skill, energy and discretion. Everything was well under way when, after eight months spent in the Takura, the expedition found itself in Sydney again. They had brought back with them some thirty tropis, tropiettes and troplets, which the Natural History Museum undertook to house for them.

Soon after his arrival, Douglas received a telephone call at his hotel, to which he paid only slight attention: it was from the Sydney *Standard*, asking for an interview the next morning. He shrugged it off as a bore: no doubt he'd have to disoblige a colleague, for he really did not feel entitled to make a statement, even less — if that was what they wanted — to write a series of articles on the tropis.

The man whom he saw come in reassured him at first: there was no question of this. His connection with the newspaper was merely of a friendly nature. For a few minutes, the talk hovered uncertainly. The man, smartly dressed and self-assured, was smiling. He kept repeating that it was Douglas he had come to see rather than any other member of the expedition because he felt sure he would find in him a man of understanding; and that such understanding would open substantial prospects for Douglas. So much so that Douglas could not help smelling something fishy behind those veiled proposals. He played up to the situation, showed all the "understanding" the other could hope for, and even a little more; with the result that, an hour later, he knew all about the Takura Development Corporation, its means and its aims, and what was expected of him: that he should help them with his knowledge of the roads, the site, and the tropis, to capture a first thousand of them.

He haggled sharply about his terms, and asked for time

83

to think it over. As soon as the man had gone, he dashed into the Greames' room. An hour later, the expedition in full strength was listening aghast to Douglas's report. The Director of the Natural History Museum had been asked to attend the meeting, together with his solicitor; and it was to the man of law that they all turned their eyes when Douglas had finished.

The lawyer at first remained silent for a while. He wrinkled his nose, rubbed it with his forefinger. Then he said:

"Well now, what *are* these tropis, after all? Apes or men?"

Pop jumped up from his seat, raising his arms to heaven. Then he went to sulk by the window, like a husband fuming over his wife's inanities.

Sybil turned towards Douglas a shaken face. This was his moment, had he wished to triumph, but he had no such thought. The pathetic appeal he could read in those lovely deep-sea eyes was soothing enough for his pride. The young woman was biting her lips with a sort of saddened rage, in which one could see regret or remorse already taking on the hue of resolution.

As for Greame, he showed some intention of replying to the solicitor. He was staring at the carpet between his feet, letting his lower lip droop rather comically over his little wrinkled Punch-like chin. At last he clicked his tongue.

"Apes or men?" he stammered, blushing. "We'd have been . . . er . . . careless and . . . er . . . guilty indeed," he admitted, "if . . . if, in the last analysis . . . it weren't . . . er . . . probably . . . impossible to say." And he looked up at the lawyer with eyes moist with anxiety.

"How so: impossible!" exclaimed the latter, his eyes agog. "The dumbest shepherd in the savanna can tell a man at first sight. Even a goitrous imbecile of the Bullarook can. If the tropi isn't recognizably human, he's an ape."

Greame sighed.

"That, you see," he said in a firmer voice, "did indeed seem so to us until today. And, in fact, between a . . . British subject and a . . . er . . . the most primitive Negrito, the biological distance is so much smaller than between the Negrito and a chimpanzee, that it enabled your goitrous shepherd to . . . to distinguish roughly an ape from a man — just as well as an anthropologist could. But conversely," he continued, with a sudden fluency that surprised them all, "conversely, it follows that an anthropologist, in turn, did not need much more insight to distinguish between the two. Why did he content himself with so rudimentary a knowledge? Because good fortune smiled on him. Good fortune, which had wiped out all the intermediate species half a million years ago. Thus our minds were lapped in a deceptive tranquillity. From that point of view," he added rather miserably, "the survival of the tropis is a calamity. It urgently poses a problem which, in our laziness, we've always been able to shelve. Namely to qualify, precisely and incontrovertibly, the specific traits of what we call Man. There was no hurry," he continued, and the sarcasm in his voice came as a surprise to his friends — "for who could have made a mistake? And we even flattered ourselves that we were thus remaining within the rational confines of science.

85

Above all, we declared, let's not stray beyond our cabbage patch! We must keep aloof from sentiments, the pitfalls of psychology, the haziness of ethics! Musn't mix our cabbages and kings!"

He sighed again.

"We felt quite smug in our ignorance, because the human species was so distinct, so well set apart from the rest of the animal kingdom that even your goitrous shepherd couldn't mistake one for t'other. If you are given very hot water, and very cold water, there's no room for doubt either. But lukewarm water, eh? What would you call it, unless you'd previously agreed on the precise number of degrees required for water to be qualified as "hot"? That's what we're up against today. Between man and the chimpanzee, no room for doubt. But between the chimpanzee and the *Plesianthropus*, between him and Peking man, between Peking man and the tropi, between the tropi and Neanderthal man, between Neanderthal man and the Negrito, and finally between the Negrito and you, dear sir — and I'm skipping not a few! — the distance each time is about the same. So if you can tell us where ape ends and man begins, we'll be very much in your debt!"

"Unless, you said, the distinction had been previously agreed upon?"

"Yes . . ."

"Well, then, can't that be done? Even if it's a bit late in the day, couldn't a congress of anthropologists be asked to supply such a definition?"

Kreps burst out laughing and slapped his thigh resoundingly.

86

"I wish you luck if you try!" he cried. "You'd be gray before they'd come to an agreement!"

"Is it so difficult, then?"

"It's not so much difficult, old man as it's arbitrary. You might as well toss for it: it would be quicker, anyway. And it would be no less exact. It's three hundred years since Locke asked, with regard to human monsters, what is the boundary between the human face and the animal; what degree of monstrosity should be fixed for refusing baptism to a child, for not granting it a soul. You see the question is not new. So you'll understand that it'll take more than three days or three months to settle a question that's been hanging fire for centuries."

The lawyer kept his eyes on Kreps absent-mindedly. Then he removed his glasses, wiped them, and put them back again.

"Well," he said, "if that's so, I'm afraid the Takura Corporation will get what they want."

"Excuse me . . ." said Sybil.

The lawyer turned to her questioningly.

"There is," she said, "a law to protect zoological species threatened with extinction. It should be possible to set it in motion."

"It might be," said the lawyer, "if the Takura Corporation intended to sell the tropis as butcher's meat. But they intend, on the contrary, to shield them from the uncertainties of the wilderness, to look after them, watch over their hygiene, their nourishment and, above all, their reproduction. It would be easy for them to prove that the law does not apply to them. The Museum could no doubt demand a special law to protect the tropis. . . . But I leave you to imagine the length of time it would take to get it enacted. Moreover, it is far from sure that it would be passed. The Takura people can pull plenty of strings, as you know. Vast interests are already at stake. No, don't you see," he said, "if it is impossible to prove that the tropis are not beasts, there's nothing to prevent their lawful owners, at the moment, from treating them like horses and elephants. In fine, either the tropis constitute the fauna of the Takura, or else they constitute its population. It's one or the other. You can't get past it."

"You've nothing to suggest?" asked Douglas, after a pause.

"I must think it over," said the solicitor. "At the moment all I see are two possible lines to take. One would be to obtain a scientific definition from some official body whose authority is unquestioned, such as the Royal Society. It would seem, according to Professor Kreps, that this can't be done. The other, then, would be to obtain a legal judgment which would *ipso facto* presuppose that the tropis are human. Thus a precedent would be established. That might not be impossible. . . ."

"For example?"

"For example . . . suppose Mr. Templemore takes a tropi into his service. . . . He doesn't pay him his wages . . . . The tropi takes legal action against him, and gets himself represented by counsel. A judgment is brought in his favor. This means that he has been recognized as having equal rights with Mr. Templemore. In other words, the rights of a human being."

"That unfortunately is impossible," said Pop, without turning round.

88

"Ah . . . Why?"

"A tropi cannot swear an oath unless he is human. It would be a sacrilege, and, incidentally, without any legal validity. Besides, how could you lawfully receive even a summons from an individual with no civil status? Vicious circle. And don't forget that the Takura people have all their wits about them."

"We're losing sight of the real problem, I feel," Willy, the surgeon, broke in gently.

They all turned towards him, except Father Dillighan who remained fiercely aloof at the window.

"After all, we're not the Society for the Prevention of Cruelty to Animals," went on Willy.

"Well?" Douglas queried, uneasily.

"If it were proved that the tropis are apes, why should we interfere? Unless we question the right of the human species to exploit the labor of domestic animals for its own benefit, on what moral grounds could we oppose the schemes of the Takura Corporation? They would then be reasonable projects: even perfectly laudable ones, since they would help to relieve the human race and spare it part of its toil. Am I right?" he asked Douglas before going on.

"Well . . . yes," said the latter guardedly.

"The Takura people's plans are criminal only if the tropis are not apes — if they too belong to the human race. And anyway, if that were proved, those schemes would automatically fall through, since slave-trading is forbidden, at least within the Commonwealth. But if, on the contrary, it is proved that the tropis *are* beasts, then, my dear friends, our duty, far from opposing the Takura

89

Corporation, will be the very opposite: to do our utmost to reduce, with the aid of the domestic tropis, the sum of human labor. It seems to me that we are letting ourselves be somewhat influenced by sentimental considerations. We have, during the last six months, got too attached to our tropis. We must make a stand against this. What should worry us, in actual fact, you see, isn't the fate of the tropis, but only the fear that we may one day wake up accomplices to a crime, if it came to be recognized that the tropis are human after all. This is not such a new problem. When America was discovered, the question arose over the Red Indians. What were those bipeds who, over there on the other side of the ocean, couldn't possibly claim to be sons of Adam and Eve? So people called them 'tailless chimpanzees' and did a roaring trade in them. All we aim at is not to make the same mistake. We aren't bound to do anything else. Agreed?" he asked, this time of the whole gathering, who at first said nothing.

"Yes," said Sybil at last, firmly.

"Well, boys," went on Willy, laughing, "we've no reason to be very proud of ourselves. Nothing easier than to find out where we stand. Sorry, Cuthbert," he said courteously to old Greame, "but for the last six months we've been thinking exclusively as anthropologists, and even as paleontologists. As if all these tropis were fossil skeletons. But they are alive, good God, they're as much alive as cats and crocodiles. They live and procreate! It's about time we started thinking as zoologists, don't you think?"

Thereupon a trumpet-major laugh burst forth from the gigantic Kreps.

"By jove!" he cried. "The egg of Columbus!"

"You might say so," agreed Willy. "What is meant by a species?" he asked. "A group of animals that can interbreed — even though outwardly they do not look alike. Thus the great Dane and the pom: they're as different from one another as a cat from a giraffe, but their union is fertile. So we classify them in the same species: that of dogs. Inversely, the lion resembles the panther, but their union is sterile. So they are of different species. You guess what I'm driving at: let's try to have a female tropi fertilized by a man. If it works, well, we'll know where we are. And so shall we if it fails."

Pop turned round. He was extraordinarily pale, and when he managed to speak, it was clear that he had some difficulty in controlling his voice. He said that if such a thing were done, he would for the rest of his days hide his own shame in his Benedictine monastery.

"But why, Pop?" exclaimed Willy. "All sorts of cross-breeding is being tried daily, by stockbreeders as well as in zoological research stations. There's nothing in it to . . . Besides, set your mind at rest," he added when he thought he understood what had outraged the priest's feelings. "You don't think for a moment I had in mind a real carnal union, actually consummated! . . . Today doctors and biologists have at their disposal technical means that deprive this kind of experiment of all equivocal or embarrassing aspects. Anyway . . ."

"Sodomy! Sodomy!" shouted Pop. "Beasts cannot sin, and there is no sin in imitating for the needs of stockbreeding or science the errings of their instincts. It is licit to create a mule, or to seek by divers crosses to create new

91

strains. But man is a divine creature. And the devious practices that you suggest merely cloak, but do not abolish, an abominable sacrilege."

"But look here, father," said Willy, "if the tropis are men, their females are women; and the sin in that case would be pardonable compared with the end pursued. I know, of course, that the Church condemns this sort of insemination, even between husband and wife. But it condemns it for family and moral reasons, and I know — from my own professional experience — that the Church does not make it a hard and fast rule, but often shuts its eyes. It seems to me that if such an experiment would help us to save from slavery . . ."

"And if the tropis are apes?" Father Dillighan cut him short.

"In that case, what harm will have been done? Nothing will come of it, and at least we shall know. . . ."

"You talk," said Pop, "as if there had never been any cases of hybridization! A bitch can be fertilized by a wolf, and the issue is a wolf dog; a she-donkey by a stallion, and even a cow by a donkey. You cannot be sure of anything. As for me, I refuse to be an accomplice to such a profanation. If you decide to do it all the same, you all will carry the sole responsibility for an inexpiable outrage."

Having thus spoken, he left the meeting without another word. The others, in silent consternation, watched him go.

Chapter 9

A LACONIC CABLE AND A SUCCINCT REPLY. AH,
WILDERNESS! . . . CONFESSION IS THE COURAGE
OF WEAKNESS. AN ATTEMPT TOO FULL OF TOMOR-
ROWS. RACIALISM MAKES ITS ENTRANCE. JULIUS
DREXLER CALLS IN QUESTION "THE ONENESS OF
THE HUMAN SPECIES." ENTHUSIASM IN DURBAN.
ARE THE NEGROES HUMAN?

A FEW weeks later, Frances, to whom Douglas had been
writing daily since his return to Sydney, was busy on a
rather long short story which she had recently under-
taken, when a cable was delivered to her. It came from
Australia and bore the laconic words:

WILL YOU MARRY ME

DOUGLAS

That was all. And it was — if not wholly unforeseen —
at least so unexpectedly sudden that her joy wilted before
wonder and alarm. She did not, perhaps, think in so many
words: "He's in danger"; but she felt dimly apprehensive
of it. She understood, too, that she must answer at once,

and without taking time to think. She lifted the receiver
to dictate an even more laconic reply:

OF COURSE

FRANCES

And, her heart at rest, she began to turn over and over
in her mind an inexhaustible variety of suppositions.

ᨅ

All except the one, of course, which six days later was
to startle and alarm her even more than she had feared.
Six days during which she received nothing — neither
letter nor wire. And then (on a Monday, a day she hated)
the letter of explanation arrived at last.

*Frances darling [it ran], so you have had my cable,
and since this morning my heart is brimming over with
your reply.*

*But though I believe — though I am certain you have
guessed that I am offering you, not happiness, but an
ordeal, I wonder whether you have guessed the extent of
it.*

*Where shall I start, Frances? No — that's not difficult:
I'm only pretending to hesitate. I must start with a confession — a pretty humiliating one.*

*Frances, during those long months spent in the wilder-
ness, I have been unfaithful to you: Sybil, yes . . . Is it a
mitigating circumstance if I add — it's true, I swear —
that my heart had no part in it? You do not know Sybil
— or hardly. I've known her since childhood. Strange
girl, strange woman. Immoral? Amoral? How to put it:
it isn't that. Her mind judges everything by its own
standards, and by them alone. It would be wrong to say*

94

that she has rejected all conventions: conventions never existed for her. At sixteen she took a lover aged thirty, whom she dominated and remodeled, and then threw over when she found out his limitations. Her marriage to old Cuthbert caused a scandal, but scandal couldn't touch her; it just died a natural death. It's not impossible that she never knew of it; it came to the same thing, anyway.

That's the woman, Frances, who calmly walked into my tent one fine starry night, a night like all others, fresh rather than hot. She said, perhaps with a touch of irony: "Doug my dear, let your mind go blank," and then her bathrobe fell away, and she enclosed me, as naturally as a shell, in the tranquil beauty of her flesh. She merely sealed my lips with one finger, murmuring: "Drink the wine simply, Douglas, when the thirst comes . . ." and she let herself glide down with a smile . . . What should I have done, Frances? And besides . . . the truth is my own senses swayed me. I too felt a little thirsty, I suppose. Will you feel less hurt, or more indignant, if I tell you that I sent out to you a silent prayer, that I secretly asked for your absolution? Be that as it may, that too is true.

But true too that this was not my only lapse. I never took the initiative in those pagan games, Frances; but when they came my way, and always with the same natural grace and simplicity, I did not shun them. Until our return to Sydney, anyway.

I'd hate to "go literary" about it now, attempt to justify myself, or implore your pardon: I'd loathe myself for it. But, what's more, it would be out of season; for though this is, to be sure, what was hardest to tell you, my love, the gravest still remains to be said.

Frances, I've come to a terrible decision. I don't know

95

where it will lead me. Actually nothing, absolutely noth-
ing, compels me to it. But what I'm going to do, somebody
had to do it. I've no leaning — you know this — towards
self-sacrifice. On the contrary, I'm dead against it. Yet if
something must be done, how can you shirk it if you are
the only one able to do it?

But I want you on my side, Frances, my darling. I want
you to share this decision. I want you to approve it. I want
us to take it, both together, as the inevitable consequence
of calm, clear thought. If what I am going to do were to
appear to you, later, as a theatrical, puerile, or romantic
gesture, I'd be too mortified.

Oh, I do want you with me, Frances, provided you still
love and respect me enough after the admission I've just
made. It's the only reason I made it for. Nothing com-
pelled me to it, either, did it? I didn't show myself a very
fine, strong, heroic fellow, but are there many men who
could throw the first stone at me? You'd have known
nothing of it and, as my father used to say, "What you
don't know, doesn't exist." I am not pleading for myself,
Frances. Quite the contrary. And I'll even make a further
admission: in all other circumstances I'd have kept that
prudent silence quite unashamedly. That's not very im-
pressive, perhaps, but I've always considered that sincerity
is at times an odious virtue, when all it can do is harm.
Yes, I'd certainly have kept silent. After all, you've never
questioned me about my private life, nor I about yours.

But it was imperative you should know my weaknesses
before I tried selling you my virtues. I have asked you to
marry me and you have accepted — but do understand
that this does not bind you in the least, *Frances. I shall*

very soon be the center of a resounding scandal, for instead of trying to smother it, there'll be several of us, myself included, doing everything to fan it. I shall no doubt come up for trial. I shall perhaps be hanged. That's what the future has in store for the man who is asking you to marry him while he is still free.

This, Frances, is what has happened . . .

At this point Frances realized that she was not grasping what she read. Her heart was seething, and in front of the words drifted the obscene image of Sybil closing round Douglas "like a shell." She read again what she had just read, straining, with a puckered brow, to wring from the words a substance that kept slipping through her fingers like quicksilver. She believed she was succeeding. She thought: "With that Sybil!" She read: *Since Saturday it is absolutely certain . . .* She thought: "Not even to have the decency . . ." She turned the page and read: *If only we had listened to Father Dillighan . . .*

. . . but who'd have thought that all the inseminations would succeed? Yes, you haven't misread, Frances: all. For since we were practically certain that a crossbreeding with man would produce no result, we tried simultaneously — as conscientious zoologists — a cross between tropis and some of the nearest ape species: chimpanzee, gorilla, orangoutang. All these crossings have succeeded.

From the angle that concerns us, the experiment is therefore a failure: it has thrown no light, it has proved nothing. The problem remains unchanged, only now it will be further complicated by the awkward problem

97

feared and foreseen by Father Dillighan: what will be those poor troplets produced by the crossbreeding with man? Yet more "in-between" creatures, more on the borderline than ever, little ape men over whom the same endless arguments will be waged . . . .

What has all that got to do with me, you'll ask?

Just this, Frances: that I shall be the father of those wretched little troplets.

I can guess your feelings: one more thing I've hidden from you. Why was I fool enough to lend myself, as a voluntary guinea pig, to this experiment! And why didn't I tell you! Because I was dimly aware of being a damn fool. And because you wouldn't have failed to tell me so. Then why did I do it nevertheless? I will try to explain.

But don't start hating Sybil, my darling; don't hate her, just because I have made you suffer on her account. She is unconscious of wrong, I believe: that's perhaps what makes her do it. But does she, really? She acts, others suffer: does the cold that freezes do wrong, or the fire that burns? She is no more conscious than they are, and the idea of evil presupposes an awareness of it.

Sybil is a woman of science to an almost monstrous degree. Nothing matters much to her mind, or in her life, save method and research. The attempt at a crossbreeding with man posited a practical problem of some gravity: absolute assurance of the donor's discretion. So it seemed to Sybil that the simplest and safest method . . . To be frank, there was no need for her even to be explicit, and when the time came I consented as a matter of course to the indispensable legal and biological safeguards. Six females, who had been isolated under supervision for five weeks, were then inseminated by Dr. Williams, according to the latest methods of gynecology. Only much later did it occur to me, with a twinge of uneasiness, that it might have been wiser, perhaps, not to limit the experiment to myself alone, but to keep the father's identity more indeterminate. The truth is, Frances, that at heart I didn't believe in it: I thought that nothing would come of it all — that the females would remain sterile.

After all, in other circumstances, this mishap might merely have amused me. But what has cropped up since, from outside quarters, no longer permits me to shrug this off lightly, even less to shirk the outcome.

It's always difficult to track down the source of a leakage. The fact is that, somehow or other, the Takura Corporation got wind of our experiment. And, later, came to know the results in their entirety. They had been lying low all this time. Now they've burned their boats.

The Natural History Museum has just been served with a legal writ summoning them to restore to the Company their lawful property of thirty tropis "together with their present and future progeny" — so runs the writ — "improperly removed from the fauna of an area ceded entirely and without reserve to the Takura Corporation." This is an obvious challenge to make us go to law: isn't that what we wanted? But the case would open very badly for us — or rather for the tropis. In the present state of the law, the case would come before a civil court, be tried on a commercial basis; and on that basis the Takura Corporation would be bound to win. We had no right to bring any animals back from the Takura, nor to make a gift of them to the Museum. We'd therefore have to get the

99

lawsuit on to our own ground, argue that the tropis don't come within the Corporation's rights, since they are not fauna, but population. But, in so doing, the Museum would automatically admit itself liable to a charge of abduction and unlawful sequestration: the Takura people, as you can well imagine, would see to it that we are all dragged in, and it wouldn't be amidst that hullabaloo of scandal and raree show that objective truth would stand the slightest chance of making itself heard. For it would be only too easy to retort that the Museum cannot seriously uphold its claim that the tropis are human, since the place of human beings is certainly even less behind iron bars than behind a weaving loom . . . . Yes, it would all end in an uproarious slapstick farce and would seal, for good perhaps, the fate of all the tropis.

The Museum's legal adviser therefore suggests they should avoid court action, and make no difficulties about acknowledging the Corporation's ownership of the tropis, while requesting them at the same time, in the interests of science, to "loan" the tropis to the Museum for a while, or even to sell them. By thus implying ipso facto *the animal nature of the tropis, they'd be granting the Corporation so substantial a point that the latter would certainly not reject this compromise. This seems to be the only course we can adopt to gain time.*

But this is not yet the worst, Frances. I am sending you herewith an article which has just come out in Melbourne, in one of the biggest Australian magazines. You will read it presently. It is signed by Julius Drexler, an anthropologist of some standing, but notoriously corrupt. He is known to live in the pocket of a big-business buc-

100

caneer in Melburne, old J.K. Pendleton, who has no more powerful rival than a certain Vancruysen. And this same Vancruysen pulls the strings behind the Takura Corporation. . . .

Now what is Pendleton's game? To ruin his rival's plans by insidiously casting doubt on the animal nature of the tropis, in an adroitly "ill-timed" article? At first sight this would seem to help us. You'll see later that it tends, on the contrary, to wreck our efforts most devilishly. For everything suggests that Pendleton's real intentions are, very probably, to launch, in his turn, an even more incredible and repulsive racket. At any rate, one thing is certain: that Drexler's article throws the door wide open to boundless abominations.

It's a Machiavellian article. Poor old Greame is beside himself: "We can't even answer back!" he says. "On paleontological grounds, the scoundrel knows jolly well he's right!" What does Drexler say in essence? That the discovery of the Paranthropus greamiensis (that's our tropis, my dear . . .) not only confirms what we know of the origins of man, but also and above all, makes a clean sweep of the notions which we had about man himself, or rather — he says (just listen to this!) — about the various species which we mistakenly lump together under this single term. For, as he goes on to show, if you want to classify the Paranthropus in the genus Homo, you grant that this genus may include four-handed creatures (not to speak of their many other simian features); if, on the other hand, you deny him inclusion among the genus Homo (as it seems, he says, some people want to), by what right, then, do we call "man" the Heidelberg fossil,

101

with its chimpanzee mandible, and the Neanderthal one which differs from the tropi only in certain structural details? And thus, step by step, why call the Grimaldi fossil human, which differs from the preceding one in a few more details only, and the Cro-Magnon, and finally the African Pygmy, the Vedda of Ceylon or the Tasmanian, whose brainpan is less developed than the Cro-Magnon's, and whose back molars still include a fifth denticle, like the great apes? The appearance of the tropis, he concludes, proves that the oversimple notion of the oneness of the human species is inept. There is no human species, there is only a vast family of hominids, in a descending color scale, with the White Man — the true Man — at the top of the ladder, and at the bottom the tropi and the chimpanzee. We must abandon our old sentimental notions, and at last establish scientifically the hierarchy of the intermediate groups "improperly called human."

Improperly called human! So here we have staring us in the face again, Frances, the grimacing ghost of racial discrimination, already to rise again, with its hellish attendants. And what discrimination, Frances! A racialism in whose name entire populations can tomorrow be stripped of their human status and the rights that go with it, and be sold, in turn, like livestock by a Pendleton! Where would the boundary be fixed, Frances? Where it pleases the strongest! *Imagine what will happen to the natives in the colonies, to the Negroes in the states where segregation is in force! And, generally speaking, to any ethnical minority!*

As a matter of fact, it has already started. All the

papers of the South African Union have reprinted Drexler's article with heavy headlines. The Durban Express *already puts the question: "Are the Negroes human?"*

So you understand, my darling, what is at issue now is not so much the fate of the tropis, or even of my little troplets. All this is likely soon to be left far behind. It's now no longer merely a question of knowing whether or not the tropis are human: that's but an interlude. It's a question of doing something that will force the whole of mankind at last to define itself, once and for all. To define itself unequivocally, irrefutably and definitively. In such a way that its rights and duties towards its members will cease to be vaguely founded on some debatable traditions, transitory sentiments, religious commandments or sectarian obligations, which can at any moment be attacked or denied; but firmly based on the clear notion of what really distinguishes man from the rest of creation.

If the distinguishing mark is that they have a soul, then it must be stated by what signs its presence or absence may be recognized.

If it's their social life, then it must be stated what signs basically distinguish primitive societies from animal societies.

If it is something else, that something must be defined.

Now, I am in a position, Frances, to demand — no, that isn't the right word: I am in a position to compel the vast and solemn institution of the British judicature to reply. And it won't be enough for them to grant or refuse the tropis the status of human beings: they will have to lay down and publicly state the grounds for their verdict.

Do you realize the scope of such a legal precedent? And that, since I — alone — am able to secure it, I have no right to shirk the issue? Even if, in the process, I risk losing my happiness, perhaps my life?

Nothing great can be achieved without risks, Frances. It's not by twiddling my thumbs that I'll shake the time-honored foundations of British justice. The deed I have to do must be as weighty.

I cannot commit such a project to the random fortune of a sheet of paper, or to the hazards of the mails. But you have already grasped that it will be painful, and hard to accomplish.

You now know everything, Frances. Will you marry me?

I love you.

DOUGLAS

Chapter 10

THE ORDER OF PRECEDENCE OF THE EMOTIONS
IN THE FEMININE HEART. A WALK IN THE RAIN.
TRIUMPH OF THE PRIMACY OF CAUSES. A STRANGE
PASSENGER. WOMEN'S FREEMASONRY. DERRY AND
FRANCES. FRANCES AND SYBIL. DERRY'S CON-
FINEMENT. FIRST DIFFICULTIES WITH THE
AUTHORITIES. FIRST CHRISTENING OF AN APE
MAN. A FUNERARY VIGIL.

WHEN Frances's eyes had come to the end of the last
line, her hands folded the letter in four, and with studied
calm she rose from the depth of the divan on which she
had been lying. Unhurriedly she arranged her hair, her
make-up, lighted a cigarette, put on a raincoat, and went
out — so she told herself — to do some shopping. But
she passed the grocer's, the butcher's and the baker's
without even turning her head, which was buried deep
in her hood. The rain was falling in a fine, dense curtain,
like the mizzle over a running tide. Through it the hills
of Hampstead Heath loomed dim and discolored. The
gravel on the narrow lane crunched under her shoes.

"Inoculated!" she thought, and she would have liked to laugh. Yes, she had imagined she was inoculated. From the last infatuation that had buffeted her life three years ago, she had, on the verge of foundering, emerged victorious in a sudden surge of will power. Poor Johnny! Flighty, fickle, destructive Johnny . . . She had said "Good-by" as usual, and even waved to him from the train window. But she had already known that she would not see him again. He had written to her every day for over a month — letters that were surprised at first, then angry, reasonable, gentle, plaintive, threatening, ironical, bitter, rageful, imploring. She did not tear them up: she read them. At first sobbing with regret and desire; but she thus took the measure of her strength and resolution. In the end she had stopped reading them: wearied and indifferent. Inoculated, she had thought with a touch of pride.

To love again? Perhaps. But suffer? Never. Can't one love without suffering? *Oughtn't* one to love without it? In love, suffering is degrading. She had never approved of her own pain. She despised the sort of women who flourish "their great aching heart" like a banner of glory.

Actually, that was the very subject of the story she had started: the tale of a woman to whom love without suffering is not real love; how can she be sure she loves unless she suffers? She feels diminished, fallen from glory. She eventually leaves the too-perfect man who gives her that too-cloudless bliss.

Inoculated . . . Had not the very serenity of her relationship with Douglas proved to her that she was at last immune? She loved him, he did not love her — or so she

106

thought — yet there had been no heartache. And when one fine day she realized that he did love her, too, he had sailed away for a year in the wake of that woman. The idiotic circumstances of his departure had made her furious, to be sure. But unhappy? Hardly. You can't call that unhappy. Then there'd been the waiting, the hard-tried patience, the ear straining for the postman, some-times anxiety, and even here and there — why deny it — a little prick, a stab of jealousy . . . . But suffering, thank God, no. Over and done with: inoculated . . . That's what she had thought . . . .

Heavy drops were dripping from the smooth leaves of the chestnut trees and landing on her hood with a soft thud.

And here I go all over again. For that wretched little hack writer! The mangled heart, and the urge to cry, and that familiar, unbearable ache in the pit of the stomach . . . . And all this for that big flabby lump of a spineless, shiftless, witless boy . . . .

She bit her handkerchief. Why, she was crying. A nice exhibition. She blew her nose wrathfully. Her right foot splashed into a puddle. She should have put on stouter shoes.

With that Sybil! That corpse-digger! And the nerve to write: "I thought of you." Idiot, idiot, triple idiot! And to start suffering again for an idiot like that! "I don't know whether you'll be less hurt or more indignant . . ." No, honestly, had anyone the right to be as fatheaded as that!

She'd not even answer him. Yes, she would! She'd write: "I thought you were different from the others.

What I loved was the wonderful trust I felt in you. You've reduced it to ashes."

She spent the next hour wandering among the trees and working out, under the finely falling rain, a farewell letter of magnificent violence. When she had finished it, she first felt a giddy emptiness, cold and gray like that dripping wall of rain. Then she thought: I haven't even mentioned his tropis. She shrugged her shoulders. The drizzle had thickened, it turned into a downpour. Frances drew the cord of her hood more tightly around her throat. Thereupon she remembered that he had written: "Maybe I'll be hanged." "What a cock-and-bull story!" she had said to herself. That tabloid journalese . . . Hanged! If he thought for a moment she'd believe . . . Anyway, why hanged? This long farrago about the tropis, she hadn't grasped the half of it. The fact was that, in spite of her commendable efforts, she had read all that part of the letter through a fog . . . . I really ought to read it again, she thought — with a first prick of remorse and anxiety. What were those last words? "A horrible and bloody project." No, he hadn't said "bloody." Nor "horrible," as a matter of fact. Why had she thought that she remembered the word "bloody"? The actual word was "painful." Why did she think of "bloody"? Fear slowly rose in her, obsessed her. She started walking more quickly towards home. "Painful and hard to accomplish": those were his exact words. To accomplish what? And why, oh why, "bloody"? She almost ran.

ↄ๏ɔ

An hour later, Frances's suffering had changed in character, without losing any of its virulence. Not that she had absolved Douglas of his betrayal. But she no longer treated him inside herself as a "little hack writer" and a "big flabby lump." She had picked up the letter to read and reread the last part. And she knew — yes, she knew well that he would do what he had said he would. What incredible animals men are! That flaccid spinelessness in front of the awful Sybil on the one hand, and that determination, that boldness on the other — for whose sake? For the tropis. At the first moment she had felt doubly insulted. Then the funny side of the situation had appealed to her. And at a last reading she eventually regained a sounder, less emotional judgment. At the same time she discovered, running through the letter from end to end, the accent of a deep, strong love: and her heart thus warmed, she could now discern in it, too, the fine fiber of generosity and exacting manliness. In short, that poor Douglas deserved, in fact, respect and even admiration, rather than scorn or anger.

So much so that, in the end, she found that the one to be scolded was herself. She had to admit that, all things put in their proper perspective, the case of the tropis with its far-reaching consequences vastly outweighed the importance of her own emotional upset. She began to feel ashamed. And with it came a sudden burst of motherly tenderness for the faithless boy and for what was, after all, but a pardonable weakness of the flesh under the desert sky . . . . Even Sybil did not go without her share in this overflow from a softened heart.

From then on, the way was open in Frances's mind to boundless anguish. With the anguish there awoke an immoderate desire to be near Douglas. He must not be left alone with his nightmares! If it turned out, alas, to be too late to stop an act of folly, she thought, she must at least be there to share the consequences. She sent a cable: *Let's get married at once,* as if this could be done over a distance of twelve thousand miles. Obstacles count for little in the plans of a woman in love. How was she to join Douglas, without money? She'd rake some up. Or Douglas would somehow wangle her coming out there. Or else they'd get married by proxy. Wasn't there some law to enable you, in an emergency, to marry by correspondence? You surely can't prevent people from marrying for the silly reason that they happen to be at the opposite ends of the earth!

Two days later she received a long cable in reply. In it Douglas announced his return to London. "Accompanied," he said. Frances's first idea was that he was coming back with Sybil, and for a moment she was wild with indignation. When she finally realized that it was probably a hint at the fact that he would be escorting the tropis, she again felt "beastly" towards him. Then it occurred to her that the absence of any hint at Sybil might possibly mean that she'd be making the trip with him, after all. The letter she received shortly after neither allayed nor confirmed her suspicions. It merely mentioned in passing that "Kreps, Pop, and the Greames are also getting ready to return." Still later Douglas stated that he would be flying back. That at first reassured Frances: it was hardly likely that one plane could contain the whole expedition, luggage, tropis and all. But, come to think of it, couldn't the party split up?

Frances was none the wiser, and none the more serene, when she found herself at last on the airfield near Slough, scanning the misty sky for the arrival of the Australian mailplane.

∽

The plane had disgorged all its passengers, and still Douglas had not appeared at the door of the cockpit. Frances had already given up hope when at last he emerged. Frances's heart gave a jump: he was not alone, a woman was on his arm . . . . But Frances quickly noticed how much smaller and plumper she was than the glamorous Sybil. "A Malay woman," she thought, for the woman was dressed in Indian fashion: a wide, draped sari of a lovely tawny hue. Afflicted with eye trouble, no doubt; why else, on such a murky day, wear those outsize dark glasses that obscured her face? Ah, married? — A last traveler was attentively holding her by the other arm.

The trio walked down the gangway and Douglas, catching sight of Frances behind the white barrier, waved his hand and smiled. The three travelers walked across the open space between the plane and the sheds. The woman, slightly bent, advanced with faltering steps, like someone whose eyesight was indeed very poor. The two men displayed towards her a really touching attentiveness.

They disappeared into the customs shed. The time they spent there seemed long to Frances. Douglas finally was the first to come out. They embraced without a word. Frances was sobbing quietly.

When — after a minute or a year? — Douglas's arms opened to release her, a hired car was waiting close by. The Malay woman and her companion were already in it. Douglas helped Frances into the car and into her seat.

111

The car moved off, and then, with a sudden, unexpected gesture, Douglas removed the sunglasses from the face in the shadow.

Frances had to stifle a cry, although she had instantly understood who that creature was that faced her. But she had not expected "that."

"That," in Frances's mind, expressed a composite feeling: that she could have taken this creature for a woman until the last moment! And that she had that face!

"She looks like Miss Merrybotham," she thought, and felt a desire to laugh that was mingled with pity. Miss Merrybotham had years ago tried to teach drawing to Frances's younger brother. All the year round she made him do water colors of holly leaves, violets and rosebuds. She sometimes added to them, with her own hand, a pretty little tit or a swallow. She never discarded a certain grave and sorrowful dignity which was ill-assorted with the mirth-provoking sound of her name: Frances remembered the giggling fits that seized her and her brother at the mere sight of that nobly mournful face. They used to suppress them behind their cupped hands, as if they were having coughing fits. . . . The little tropi female had Miss Merrybotham's face. She had, above all, her expression.

"What do you think of her?" Douglas was asking meanwhile.

Actually, apart from that first impression, Frances at that moment was little concerned with forming opinions: her head and heart were brimming over with questions. But how could she ask all those questions in front of that stranger? ("This is Mimms," Douglas had said, "from the Sydney Museum.")

"She looks like Miss Merrybotham," she said, and explained why. "You had no trouble?"

"You bet, my pet!" laughed Douglas. "We needed eleven visas and a cartful of vaccination certificates: you know the sort of acrobatics it takes to round them up for an ordinary individual. So imagine what it was like for a fictitious woman: had we declared her as an animal, we'd never been allowed to take her with us. Luckily during the war I was parachuted six times into occupied territory: so forged papers are my stock in trade!"

"What about her, during the trip?"

"She behaved like a lady," said Douglas with a smile of tenderness.

The tropiette, motionless and well-mannered in her seat, kept looking up at Douglas every few moments, with expectant, submissive, eagerly questioning eyes. Douglas smiled at her, and pulled out of the traveling bag at his feet a sandwich wrapped in greaseproof paper. She followed his every movement, like a dog at the master's table, hoping to get a scrap. With a jerk Douglas bounced the sandwich on his forearm, like a ball, caught it in the air, and the tropiette broke into a brief, childish peal of laughter, which revealed strong, white, pointed teeth and four impressive eyeteeth. Douglas held out the sandwich to her. She stretched out a swarthy hand, with long, tapering fingers ending in nails that had been cut to a point and varnished red. "Her hands are more beautiful than mine," thought Frances, and she felt queerly moved. She watched her massively grinding the sandwich with the mournful dignity of Miss Merrybotham eating a cream bun. Douglas said to Frances: "Her name's Derry," and

113

the tropiette, on hearing her name, left off chewing. "She has the same glance as van Gogh in his self-portrait with the pipe," thought Frances. "Unless it was van Gogh who," she reflected, "on the brink of insanity, had tropi eyes . . . ." Douglas said: "Give," and Derry handed him the end of her sandwich. Douglas passed the bread and ham to Frances, then smiled at the tropiette with a nod of encouragement. She looked attentively, two or three times, from Douglas to Frances, and at last uttered a sound between *bliss* and *preeze*, which was sufficiently like the word *please* to make Frances promptly hand her the sandwich. Derry had already plunged her teeth into it, but Douglas said, "Tut, tut!" rather sternly, and she pronounced, "Zankyou," and burst into the same brief, childish laughter as before. But the next moment her face had already resumed its pathetic expression of woeful dignity.

"Take that veil off her head," Frances suggested, and Douglas complied. Derry immediately lost all resemblance to Miss Merrybotham, and assumed an equivocal countenance: half she-monkey, half sailors' moll. The reason was, no doubt, that mop of hair that fell in fringes down to her eyebrows. Under that mane the forehead, no longer concealed by the veil, could be seen to be abnormally low; whereas the pointed, velvety ears, that moved in time with her chewing, peeped too high up through the strands of hair.

"Where are we going?" Frances suddenly exclaimed in surprise.

The car had just left the main road that leads to London via Hammersmith, and turned right, into the road to

Windsor. Douglas smilingly took Frances's hand and pressed it.

"The Royal Society of Anthropology has rented a small house for us, in Surrey. A lovely cottage deep in the woods, surrounded by a sheltering garden. Anyway," he added with a laugh, "that's how I imagine it."

"For . . . Derry and you?"

"For Derry and *us*, who — unless you have an objection, darling — will be getting married tomorrow."

"Tomorrow, Douglas!"

"Why not, Frances? Haven't we waited long enough?"

Although the gentleman named Mimms had, ever since the start of the journey, kept his eyes glued to the landscape with dogged tact, Frances did not dare hug Douglas.

"Let's make the most of these few months," he said. His voice suddenly sounded husky and a little muffled.

It was Frances now who gripped his hand, but unsmilingly, with anxious fervor. She turned a questioning, strained face towards Douglas. The corners of her mouth drooped and quivered.

"Later," murmured Douglas.

The purring engine, the jolting road had sent Derry to sleep. She had slumped back, her head finding the welcome support of Mimm's shoulder to rest her cheek on. Her eyelids were brown and silky, with very thick long lashes. The delicate folds of her mouth had dropped half open over the bulging jowl, giving a glimpse of the mighty eyeteeth. One of the high-set ears lay bare. It was the tint of a ripe apricot. The whole sleeping face expressed a gentle sadness blended with disturbing cruelty.

∽

Frances and Douglas got married, not on the next day, but eleven days later, when they could at last pay a flying visit to London.

They had had some trouble in getting Derry settled. What was going on in that mysterious little skull? In Sydney she had seemed to get used to living alone — away from the other tropis — during the period of isolation that preceded her fecundation. She had attached herself first to Mimms, then even more to Douglas, much as a faithful bitch might. Wherever they were, she seemed to be happy. However, during the first night spent at Sunset Cottage, Mimms, awakened by a draught of fresh air, found the window open and the room empty. Derry was eventually located in the garden, hidden between the yews and the garden fence, which she had been unable to climb.

Frances listened, with amused patience, to the two men floundering in vain conjectures. At last she broke in with the gentle assertion:

"She's jealous."

"Of whom?" exclaimed Douglas.

"Of me. . . . We women have a way of understanding one another," she added with a falsely sweet smile.

Douglas flushed to the tips of his ears.

"You haven't forgiven me?" he asked when they were alone. "I could have kept my mouth shut," he argued in his defense, as he had done in his letter.

"I'd only have had to look at you, poor darling, when mentioning Sybil's name, to know everything. Still, the question now is Derry. Do you think she'll get used to it?"

"To what?"

"To my presence."

116

"Do you seriously think she's jealous?"

No doubt was possible. Not that Derry manifested the slightest hostility towards Frances. On the contrary, she soon seemed to get as much attached to her as to the two men. What she could not bear was that Douglas and Frances should both be out of her sight together. She would then become restive and moody, go shuffling around the house, opening doors. The second night, when Douglas and Frances had retired, Mimms tied Derry's wrist to his with a piece of string. But Derry, on her mat, tossed around so much that he could not sleep a wink.

The countertest proved conclusive: Douglas spent the next night near the tropiette, and she went to sleep without fuss. Frances took Douglas's place: Derry slept just as soundly. Mimms took up his post again, with the cord tied to his wrist: in the morning the cord was there, but the tropiette had gone. She had managed to release herself, undo the lock, and find Douglas's room. There she was found fast asleep on his bedside rug.

The household had to be organized differently. A small bedroom was made out of the bathroom. This communicated with the two large bedrooms: one was the keeper's, the other was Douglas's room (later the young couple's). Every night, Derry went quietly to sleep in her little room provided Douglas left his door open. Once she was asleep he could close it; but if Derry was the first to awake in the morning, she would, without formality, walk into his room, as if to check that he was alone. Douglas would turn her out, and she would go back to sleep on her mat without more ado.

However, after the wedding, when she found Frances next to Douglas, nothing could persuade her to leave the

117

room. She stretched out on the rug beside the bed and refused to budge: it was obvious she would rather let herself be killed on the spot. This scene recurred every day. And Frances was doubtless wise to persuade Douglas to bow to the inevitable. He wanted to lock the door, but had Derry noticed it, the discovery would probably have set them right back to the starting point.

Frances amused herself with the tropiette like a little girl with her doll. It was she who attended to Derry's toilet — she considered it more seemly: Derry had a too feminine appearance in her bath, in spite of — or because of — her fine dove-colored fur and, above all, her pink breasts. And she had to be bathed every day, for she quickly exuded a pervasive animal smell. In the beginning, Frances used to soap her herself. But Derry showed a really too sensual appreciation of this caress: closing her eyes, cooing softly, and seeming almost on the brink of fainting. Frances very quickly taught her to soap herself, and almost cried with laughter at the sight of Derry's four-handed manipulations: soaps, sponge and brush would pass from one hand to the other in a sort of clownish jugglery. Derry laughed too, to see Frances laughing.

In London, Frances had bought all kinds of material to make dresses for Derry. Or rather Indian saris: in Western dress, the bent posture and long arms were too suggestive of an ape in disguise. Derry visibly enjoyed dressing herself up, and even revealed signs of budding coquetry: when the choice was left to her, she invariably selected the reddest material. Her coquetry, though, did not extend to ornaments: Frances vainly tried to interest her in trinkets. Derry would finger them for a moment, but soon laid them aside. The question of shoes proved

118

insoluble: Derry could not stand them, and would hobble about in them, as if crippled. She could not even get used to sandals which, anyway, stressed rather than concealed the fact that her feet were actually hands.

One day Frances tried make-up on her. The result was deplorable. The lipstick on her jowl only emphasized her lack of lips, and the rouge on her cheeks brought out their lines and wrinkles: Derry suddenly looked more aged than the fifty-six-year-old Miss Merrybotham.

Derry's presence and the problems it raised for Frances and Douglas had, as can be seen, somewhat disturbed their "honeymoon." It was rather as if their wedding trip had been encumbered by some orphaned niece, moody and ailing to boot. It cost them the joys of solitude *à deux*; in exchange, they were spared its disadvantages: the difficult adjustment of outlook and temperament during the trying running-in stage. Moreover, the rare moments they were able to snatch from that troublesome tyranny assumed a precious character which they cherished with fervor. A fervor made up of a curious mixture of carefreeness and despair. For Frances knew now that their happiness would not last. A short-term happiness which, being without hope, must be enjoyed without thought. Frances was no longer in ignorance of any detail of Douglas's scheme. "You'll never dare!" she had cried at first. But he had said quietly: "Every day thousands of people drown their dog's or cat's litter. They don't like doing it, yet they do it." "But *they* are puppies or kittens!" — His answer had been: "Well?"

It had taken her long to decide whether or not she approved. She never mentioned her doubts to her husband: his decision was taken, her own qualms would only have worried him needlessly. And gradually, as she gained a deeper insight into Douglas's reasons, and into the consequences of his act, she came to accept this act, then to approve it, and finally to agree with it no longer passively, but with all her heart. A torn and anguished heart, but one ready to bear the ordeal to come.

In the meantime, the whole expedition — Kreps, Pop, and the Greames — had returned by boat, bringing with them some twenty tropis, male and female, including all those that had been variously inseminated. This had meant signing an agreement with the Takura Corporation, as they had done for the others. The agreement specified that any progeny could be claimed by the Corporation. Douglas had insisted on their accepting this condition: it well suited his purposes.

The Royal Society of Anthropology had agreed to Greame's request that the tropis' arrival in London should be kept secret, and that to him should be reserved the honor — which was indeed his by rights — of being the first to speak of the *Paranthropus erectus* in the press and scientific journals. Julius Drexler's lack of etiquette had, happily, aroused among the Fellows of the Society unanimous censure, which was to Greame's benefit.

In this way, by the time Derry and her companions were due for confinement, nothing of importance had yet leaked out either among the general public or in scientific or business circles. Thus Douglas had his hands as free as he had wished.

Dr. Williams came by air from Sydney for the confinements. The births all occurred within a few days of each

120

other, at the Whipsnade Zoo, where an emergency clinic had been set up. The only exception was Derry, who was delivered by Willy at Sunset Cottage, according to plan.

Greame and his wife, notified by telephone, rushed down from London. Two months previously, Sybil had turned up at the cottage one day when she knew she would find Frances alone. When she left, Frances cheerfully admitted defeat. It is quite true, she thought, that conventional feelings simply break down in the face of such a woman. Sybil's frankness, gaiety, vital strength, and the genuine affection she promptly showed towards Frances swept stale grudges away like a mountain torrent. Frances had made an effort to think: "Those hands have touched Douglas, have caressed him. Those lips have kissed him" — but it definitely was an effort, and no images rose to her mind. On the contrary, Frances at times caught herself — quite suddenly — being stirred by a wave of spontaneous, subtly fraternal affection . . . . Above all, it was patently obvious that Sybil did not claim, nor ever had claimed, the slightest right to Douglas, so that Frances felt safer with her — she had to admit — than she might feel in the future with less forthright women.

She did not always, subsequently, cherish such noble sentiments toward Sybil. It would happen that the obscene image of Sybil "like a shell" would surge up from a smile, a gesture or a word. But it quickly vanished. The torrent once more swept all before it, leaving on its banks nothing but the clear, crisp sand. At other times Frances found hard to bear the all too natural — that is: too oblivious — attitude which Douglas displayed in

Sybil's presence. It was quite true that Douglas felt perfectly at ease. As so often happens, he had been the first to grant himself an unqualified pardon.

ow

What Frances had all along hoped for, deep in her heart, was that the birth of a too human-looking tropi would shake Douglas's resolution.

Now the newborn was there before them asleep. At first glance he looked like all newborn babies, reddish, wrinkled and grimacing. But he was apricot-colored and covered with a fair, silky down, "like pig's bristles," said Willy. He had four hands, little overlong arms, outstanding and too high-set ears, the head planted too far forward. Greame opened the baby's mouth, and said that the jaw formed a more open *U* than in real tropis; the browline was perhaps a trifle less marked; the skull . . . too early to pronounce on it. Nothing to go on, all told.

"No room for doubt?" asked Douglas.

"None," said Greame. "He's a tropi."

Frances remained silent. She felt two cool arms around her — Sybil's. She let herself be taken into the next room, and stayed there for a long time, now and then convulsively pressing her friend's hand in hers. Neither of them spoke. But that hour, passed in silence, put the final seal to their friendship.

This was but a passing weakness. The next morning it was Frances who dressed the baby — swaddled it, wrapped it in a quilted shawl, covered its downy little head with a bonnet, and placed it in Douglas's arms as she would have done with their own child.

122

An hour later, Douglas presented himself at the Guild-ford registry office, to have the child entered under the name of Garry Ralph Templemore. Matters proceeded smoothly enough until it came to entering the particulars of the child's mother. Never in all his life, the registry clerk maintained, had he been asked to put on a birth certificate: "mother: unknown."

"It's against the law!" he doggedly kept repeating.

"The child exists," Douglas pointed out patiently. "You wouldn't refuse it a legal status if it couldn't claim a lawful father?"

"No . . ."

"You'd put: 'father: unknown,' wouldn't you?"

"Ye-es, but . . ."

"Well, this one can't claim a lawful mother. So you'd better put 'mother unknown.'"

"But the mother *can't* be unknown, dash it all! She must have been about when the child was born! She must exist, be known, have a name, and all that!"

"I told you: she's called Derry."

"That isn't a full name. What about her other particulars, anyway?"

"She hasn't any. She's a native woman, I'm telling you."

From this prolonged wrestling bout, Douglas emerged the winner on points. The clerk, eventually worn out, entered the mother as "native woman known as Derry," and Douglas left the registry office, the birth certificate in his pocket.

His next visit — this time with the baby in his arms — was to the vicarage. A plump, kindly housekeeper showed

123

him into the parlor, where he was kept waiting for a few minutes. The vicar apologized when he appeared at last: "Can't be up with the lark any more, I'm afraid. Awful fits of giddiness. My liver, you know: it's fallen out with my kidneys, stirring up trouble with the stomach, till the whole poor old constitution is undermined by anarchy . . . . Persuading them to love each other is no less difficult, I find, than persuading my parishioners. . . . However . . . Lovely baby," he added, absent-mindedly, peeping under the baby's shawl. "You've come about a christening, I suppose?"

"Yes, sir."

"You're new to this parish, I take it? Quite so. You needn't have troubled, you know, to bring the child along. I shall be very glad to come round to your house to discuss the arrangements with you and the happy young mother."

"If you don't mind, sir, I should like the christening to take place at once."

"At once!" exclaimed the vicar, looking at Douglas with surprise. "This is very — unusual, Mr. . . . er . . ."

"Templemore. Douglas Templemore. I know, sir, but there are special circumstances which oblige me."

"I see. . . . Well, seeing you've brought the child . . . we'll go round to the church. The godparents are waiting there, I suppose?"

"No," said Douglas, "I'm alone."

The vicar let go of the door handle.

"Oh!" he said, coming closer. "No doubt you intended to . . . I am listening, my son."

"I have only recently got married, and this child was born out of wedlock."

124

The vicar's face, with consummate art, conveyed severity, understanding, indulgence.

"I would like the ceremony to be surrounded by the greatest possible discretion," said Douglas.

The vicar nodded, with closed eyes.

"I myself wish to be godfather, and I was wondering whether your housekeeper, perhaps, would be kind enough to . . . that is, if you agree, sir . . ."

The vicar's eyes were still closed.

"It is highly desirable," continued Douglas, "that my wife and I be the only ones to know. . . . She has accepted the child's existence with great nobility of heart. It's up to me to see that she need not suffer publicly . . . from . . ."

"We shall do as you wish, Mr. Templemore," said the vicar. "Please wait here for a moment."

He soon returned, accompanied by the kindly housekeeper. They all proceeded to the church. The old woman held the child over the font. She would have liked to please Douglas by saying, "Isn't he just like you!" but truly, she had in a long life seen many an ugly newborn babe, but one such as this . . . The child was duly christened Garry Ralph.

"Father's name?"

"Douglas M. Templemore."

"Mother's?"

"She only has a Christian name. She's a New Guinea native."

"Ah . . ." thought the old woman. "So that's it. . . ." She looked again at the sleeping child in her arms, tried to imagine the face he would have later. She saw him at a public school, among scoffing schoolfellows. "Poor mite ... won't they bully him ..."

The vicar's pen was still poised over the register. He was twisting it a dozen times between his fingers, in hesitant perplexity. His face now ill-concealed his profound disapproval. At last he wrote, saying as he did so:

"... a ... native ... woman ..."

He made Douglas and the godmother sign the register, then closed it without a word. Douglas held out a handful of notes: "For your good works." The vicar inclined his head without breaking his grave silence. Douglas amply rewarded the weakly protesting godmother, retrieved the child, and with it on his arms, turned back towards Sunset Cottage.

Douglas and Frances spent the afternoon near the cot, watching the sleeping child. To give herself courage, Frances scanned the little red face for every possible sign of its animal nature. And indeed they were numerous. Apart from the high-set ears, the forehead was receding, and in its center the embryo of a brow ridge could be seen raising the skin; the little mouth protruded like a snout; the large, chinless lower jaw joined the upper one in a jutting protuberance; the shoulders seemed to run, behind the ears, straight into the skull, without any neck.

And yet, in spite of her efforts to hold on to these features, Frances could not help regarding the little creature before her as a human child. Twice he woke up and cried, the little tongue quivering in his wide-open mouth. He waved his little hands with their rosy fingernails. Frances gave him the bottle. Her heart was heavy. The child sucked greedily and went to sleep.

At dusk Douglas and Frances had a light meal. Then they walked along the hedge-flanked country lane, arm in arm, their hands clasped, their fingers intertwined. From time to time Frances brushed her cheek against Douglas's, or touched his hand with her lips. When night had fallen completely, they decided to go in.

At the foot of the stairs, she threw her arms round Douglas for a long moment. Then, in spite of her reluctance, she went up to bed as she had promised she would. She swallowed a draught to make herself sleep.

Douglas sat down at his desk and started to write. He put on paper a complete record of events. From time to time he broke off, and went to smoke a cigarette in the garden, all a-murmur in the summer night, or else had a pipe, deeply ensconced in one of the vast leather armchairs; then he would go back to work.

Towards four he had finished. He opened the window wide on to a sky paling with the first gleam of dawn. The child woke and started to cry. Douglas warmed a bottle. The child drank it and fell asleep again. Douglas returned to the window. He watched the sky turn mauve, then pink. Before the sun had risen, he closed the window again. He lifted the telephone receiver and asked for Dr. Figgins, of Guildford. He apologized for troubling him at such an early hour, but it concerned, he added, a fatal case.

The hypodermic syringe was in the drawer, with the blue bottle labeled in red and black. He slowly filled the needle. His fingers did not tremble.

Chapter 11

WHEN Douglas's trial came up at the Old Bailey, in
October, he had already won the first round: public
opinion was aroused. Not that it was unanimously on his
side, far from it. But the newspapers were full of the case
which supplied a major topic of conversation in Tooting
and Chelsea, in Oxford and in Newcastle. Even Paris
started talking about it, New York cocked an ear. No one
could any longer try to suppress the case or disregard it.

It all began with the photographs of Derry, her com-
panions and their offspring, featured in the *Daily Picture*.
The Londoners' love of all animals is well known.
(Brumas, the Zoo's baby polar bear — "Have you seen

128

Brumas?" — attracted more than a million visitors within a few weeks.) Everybody wanted to form his own opinion of the tropis. But Vancruysen did not lack foresight, and his arm was almost as long as that of the law: hardly had the tropis arrived in London, when the Ministry of Health decreed that they must be put in quarantine, and instructed the Zoo to stop exhibiting them to the public. But the Yorkshire mill-owners were no less influential. Once the photos had appeared in the *Daily Picture*, letters of protest — as had been foreseen — came pouring in by the thousands; and the government, questioned with caustic humor by an old Labor member in the House of Commons, lifted the ban. This produced such a rush that, just as for Brumas, relief services had to be run on Sundays on the bus route to the Zoo. Soon the tropis' success with the public far outstripped that which the polar bear had enjoyed. The great debate became general: were these creatures men or apes? Was Douglas a criminal or a public benefactor? Faithful old friends would fall out over him; engagements were broken off.

Shortly before the opening of the trial, the *Evening Tribune* summed up the heated argument in the succinct words:

ROPE OR RIBBON FOR DOUG TEMPLEMORE?

This headline appeared over an account of the rumpus that had broken up a meeting at the Kingsway Hall, organized by the Animal Lovers' Guild.

After dispatching the normal business — the newspaper reported — the lady chairman had risen. In a voice quivering with emotion she had said:

"In a few weeks' time begins the trial of a hero. We

129

must not seek in any way to influence the verdict. We are not even entitled, as you know, to give public expression to our feelings without risk of contempt of court. But who can prevent us from already now putting forward Douglas Templemore's name for a public distinction? Might not that subsequently have some weight in the balance of justice? What is the opinion of this meeting?"

A little lady got up and said she did not quite understand. What service had this man rendered? Had he not killed his child?

"He has sacrificed that little creature," declared the lady chairman, "for the weal of its brothers, doomed like him by the infamous Takura Company to a life of utter misery and odious bondage. Which of us would not put away our own cat, our faithful dog, rather than let the poor animal fall into the clutches of a villain? Now, don't we all know what fate awaited those delightful animals — a fate which, alas! still threatens them — had not Douglas Templemore, by a heroic gesture sacrificed himself for them!"

A gentleman in the audience then rose. He was tall and spare, with a thick, ginger mustache. He said:

"The lady chairman refers to the tropis as 'those animals.' First, to consider them as such is playing straight into the hands of those who are only waiting to treat them as beasts of burden. Secondly, if they *are* animals, why should our society intervene? Nobody intends to ill-treat them. Unless the lady chairman holds that it amounts to maltreatment of animals to make them do what millions of men are being made to do. Thirdly and lastly, I too have seen these tropis. I have seen them

130

chipping stones, fitting steel frames, playing among themselves. And I have the honor to tell the lady chairman that they are men, just like her and me. And the shape of their toes won't make me change my mind! As for Templemore, well, he's murdered his son: and that's the long and short of it. Even if he'd had him by a mare or a goat, he'd still be his son. And I say that if they now let you drown your kids like puppies, it will soon be the end of England. That's why I vote for him to be hanged!"

Having had his say, he was about to sit down. He wasn't given the time. Half a dozen ladies, peaceful enough to look at, had suddenly closed in on him, all fangs and claws. Men, those graceful, frail and gentle little things? Men, those adorable pets? Let him only dare repeat it!

Whereupon other persons, in their turn, tried to remind those irate ladies that their misguided show of affection was positively wrecking the tropis' chances, for, as everyone was talking himself black in the face telling them . . .

They couldn't finish the sentence. The irate ladies received reinforcement. In a moment the entire audience split into two hostile camps, each claiming the tropis for the rival species of man or beast. In vain did the lady chairman, utterly overwhelmed, brandish her shrill little bell in despair. The police had to be called in to clear the hall.

There was, too, an open letter, signed by "The Association of Christian Mothers of Kidderminster," and published in *The Times*, which caused quite a stir.

"Sir," the letter began, "we ask for the hospitality of your columns to appeal publicly to His Holiness, the

131

Pope, and His Grace, the Archbishop of Canterbury . . ."

And it went on to put, in essence, the very question that had for so long been racking Father Dillighan: could one, should one refuse the baptismal sacrament to the five little troplets in the Zoo? The thought that these little beings had not even been privately christened "worried their consciences as mothers and Christians." It "troubled their sleepless nights." They therefore begged those high ecclesiastical authorities to make a pronouncement as to whether or not these little beings should be received within the Community of Christ.

The Vatican remained silent. The Archbishop replied, in a letter generally deemed embarrassed, "that this case did indeed raise a grave problem which must concern and perplex all Christian consciences; but that, according to his information, the nature of the tropis was likely to constitute an important element in a trial soon to come before the courts and that, the matter thus being *sub judice,* any expression of opinion would be definitely out of place."

So the trial was about to open, as can be seen, in a rather feverish atmosphere. Yet Douglas, who had at first rejoiced to see the British public warm to the tropis' fate with such passion, began to fear that this very passion might succeed only in obscuring the real issue.

A great number of letters arrived for him every day at the cottage in the Vale of Health; Frances brought them to him at Brixton prison. Most of them were encouraging, a few abusive; but nearly all of them aroused his anger. "Those fools are on the right road, but for the wrong reasons!" he would exclaim.

132

"What wrong reasons?" Sybil, who sometimes accompanied Frances on her visits to the prison, asked him one day. "It seems to me, on the contrary . . ."

"They muddle everything!" said Douglas impatiently. "As if I'd only killed that little creature to please our dumb friends' dumber friends! As for the others, all they see in me is some damn fool of a victim. Do you know what one of these fatheads has written to me? 'You are another Dreyfus!' . . . Must I get myself hanged to make them understand what it's all about?"

In the meantime there was hardly anyone, Sybil included, who did not get on his nerves.

"What have I done to upset Douglas?" she asked Frances. "I can't open my mouth any more without his snapping my head off!"

"You must forgive him," said Frances. "He's staking his life, don't forget."

"I'm not forgetting it," protested Sybil. "And for heavens' sake, don't you get angry too!" she begged, as she saw Frances growing pale. "Better tell me what brick I've dropped."

"I'm not angry. I'm scared," Frances confessed. "Scared for him. And he is scared, too, after all. And if he gets angry it is because you happen to talk like the people who, he says, will put the rope round his neck."

"I don't see how," said Sybil.

"By making light of the trial. The outcome most people expect — and you too, Sybil, though you may not admit it — is a vague *status quo*. They would certainly like the tropis to be left in peace, and Douglas to be acquitted, too. The rest they'd rather leave alone."

133

"What rest? The decision as to whether the tropis are human or not?"

"Yes. At heart, people find that disturbing, you see. And you too. Don't say you don't."

"It doesn't disturb me at all. I merely go on thinking that it is unscientific."

"It amounts to the same. If Douglas feels the jury think as you do, or as do those other people, that they shirk going to the bottom of the matter, he'll stick out his neck so recklessly that they'll just *have* to make up their mind — even if it costs him his head."

"That would be a fool's game!"

"But he'd play it. And I can't blame him, even though at the mere thought of it, my heart misses a beat. I've no more respect than he has for those halfhearted gamblers who boldly stake a fortune on one throw, then quickly try to withdraw their stake, when no one's looking . . . . Do you think he could bear the thought of having killed that little creature — if it should now turn out to have been all for nothing? That he'd stroll out of the court, his hands in his pockets, thanking the judge for his leniency? That would be too heart-rending a defeat."

"A certain Don Quixote, too, didn't want to take back his stake. The tropis couldn't be nicer, I grant you. But the whole lot of them just aren't worth the life of a man like Douglas."

Frances shrugged her shoulders and said gently:

"All that's so far away already."

"What is?"

"The fate of the tropis. It's funny you don't understand, Sybil."

134

"But what does he expect of the trial, then?"

"Nothing that you can put in so many words, it's true. Indeed, it's possible nothing at all will come of it. You can't tell beforehand."

"Why, then, that's madness!"

"Maybe it is. But maybe, too, it'll lead to all sorts of things we cannot foresee. How can you tell if you don't try? You remember the captain in *Typhoon?*"

"Yes . . . no . . . why?"

"Because Douglas takes after him . . . . Should he avoid the cyclone? the captain wonders. Wouldn't it be the wisest course, both for his ship and his own skin? But he thinks of his owners: 'Expensive trip!' they'll say. 'That's a lot of fuel you've burned.' And I'll say: 'I went two thousand miles off my course to avoid some heavy weather.' 'My word!' they'll say. 'Must have been deucedly heavy weather!' 'As for that,' I'll say, 'I can't tell, since I kept out of it.' That's why he plunges straight into the hurricane. . . ."

"And Douglas will do the same. . . . Definitely!" Sybil sighed, "I'll never get the hang of people like that. What good can come of it all?"

"I don't know. . . . Something like . . . new 'good tidings,' perhaps. . . . Look, Sybil, you yourself . . . you believe in neither God nor the devil, I know. But still, a word like the soul, does it really mean nothing to you?"

"Why no," said Sybil, "it does. As to everybody else. On one condition, though: that someone first explains to me what it is. Or rather by what *sign* it can be recognized."

"That's exactly what Douglas says!"

135

"No doubt," smiled Sybil. "I prompted him."

"But that's just it, Sybil: what is that sign? Have you an answer?"

"If there were one, we'd have heard of it."

"Well, isn't it odd that we haven't?" asked Frances eagerly. "Why, everyone's agreed that a saucer-lipped negress though, in intelligence, she be a hundred times closer to a chimpanzee than to Einstein, still shares with Einstein something irreplaceable that the chimpanzee lacks. Call it soul or what you will. But by what sign, as you say, Sybil, do we know that it is so? Isn't it absolutely incredible, after all the ages men have been arguing about it, that we still have not found a reply? That we haven't been able to agree on that indisputable sign? Don't you think so?"

"Yes . . . perhaps . . ."

"You pride yourself on being an 'immoralist,' Sybil. But if you are, mightn't it be for the very reason that there is no such apparent sign? If that sign were clearly recognizable, would it not be a yardstick for all your actions?"

Sybil seemed sunk in thought before making up her mind to reply.

"Perhaps," she said. "You are touching a sore spot there Frances. — one that I usually cover up quite well . . . ." Her tone of voice changed oddly. "An immoralist . . . yes, I am that. But I don't 'pride' myself on it, believe me. I'm not unaware, you know, of what people often think of my life. . . . But what you probably don't know is that there are times when it makes me very miserable. Not what people think of me, good Lord no! But that this

136

life of mine depends so utterly on me, on me alone . . .
on my sole judgment. . . . It makes me giddy at times
. . . panicky. You're surprised, Frances? You thought me
less vulnerable, more bulletproof? Nobody's bulletproof:
our armor is never more than tinfoil. The heavens are
empty, Frances. But though you know it's so, you still
can't get used to it. Can't get used to the sheer meaning-
lessness of one's acts . . . to the fact that good deeds, bad
deeds prove quite haphazardly boons or banes . . .
God is always silent, always. All that we can found good
and evil on are the quicksands of our own intentions. . . .
Nothing ever comes to guide us. . . ." She sighed. "It's
not much fun, day in, day out."

"And supposing," said Frances gently, "supposing
Douglas could compel people to answer . . . to disclose, to
reveal at long last that *sign*, that distinguishing mark that
the tropis must show to be admitted among us, among the
members of that human freemasonry which requires, as
qualification for membership — a soul. Wouldn't our
acts, all our *human* acts, Sybil, automatically be founded
on such a sign? Founded no longer on the quicksands of
our intention, as you say, on the intangible phantoms of
good and evil, but on the changeless granite of what we
are . . . . Wouldn't that spell rest, Sybil, even for you,
and peace, and a guide at last?"

"What we are . . ." murmured Sybil.

"Whether we want it or not," said Frances softly, with
a touch of melancholy.

"What we are . . ." said Sybil again.

"This side of good and evil," said Frances.

"What we are . . ." Sybil was saying. "We could really

137

know it?" she added in a sudden schoolgirl voice, touchingly fresh and simple. "Do you think we could?" she asked Frances in that schoolgirl voice.

"If we can know it for the tropis, that will mean we can know it for ourselves, Sybil," said Frances. "But if that's to come about you must not . . . you must not think of Douglas as a Don Quixote. You must trust in him to the very end," she whispered in a voice in which faith and anguish mingled. "Even if we should all be dead before we saw the fruit of his sacrifice . . . After all," she added more firmly, "it wouldn't be the first time! Not the first time that the oaks of Dodona seem at first to be talking only to the deaf . . . until, one day, the faint rumor bursts into a paean of hope."

Chapter 12

DR. FIGGINS'S PROFESSIONAL CONSCIENCE. SOME
LIGHT ON CROSSBREEDING, HYBRIDIZATION, AND
EVEN ON TELEGONY. DR. BULBROUGH'S PRUD-
ENCE. PROFESSOR KNAATSCH'S ASSERTIONS. "THE
ASTRAGALUS: THAT'S MAN." PROFESSOR EATONS'S
COUNTERSTATEMENTS. DISPUTES ABOUT THE
UPRIGHT POSTURE. "MAN HAS HANDS BECAUSE
HE THINKS." PROFESSOR EATONS COMES TO
STRANGE CONCLUSIONS.

D R. Figgins!"

He was the first witness called by the prosecution. The
doctor stepped into the witness box and took the oath. Mr.
Justice Draper, beneath his hot white wig, discreetly
wiped his brow. The early October day was oppressive
with a sultry, thundery heat. The court was filled to
overflowing.

Sir C. W. Minchett, Q.C., counsel for the prosecution,
opened fire.

"Dr. Figgins, I shall ask you to reply to my questions
briefly and without unnecessary comment," he said. "It
appears that at 5 a.m. on the 7th of June, you were sum-

moned by telephone and promptly went to Sunset Cottage?"

"Yes."

"Would you tell us in your own words what you found there?"

"A small dead body in a cot."

"The body of a newborn male child?"

"Yes."

"So what did you do?"

"Examined it — and called the police."

"Were you able to establish the cause of death?"

"Yes: death had resulted from an injection of five centigrams of strychnine chlorhydrate."

"Would that dose be instantaneously fatal even to a large animal?"

"It would."

"Did the accused inform you that he had himself given the injection that morning, and had done so deliberately?"

"He did."

"Were you able to ascertain whether his statement was correct?"

"I was. It was confirmed by my examination and by the post-mortem performed by the police surgeon in my presence."

"Are you quite satisfied that death could not have been due to any other cause?"

"Quite."

"Were you, moreover, shown a declaration, signed by Sir Selby D. Williams, of the Royal Australian College of Surgeons, to the effect that the prisoner was beyond doubt the victim's father?"

"Yes."

"Have you any reason to doubt Sir Selby's authority, or the truth of his statement?"

"I have not."

"In short, have you any reason to doubt that the accused is both the father of the deceased and the author of his death?"

"No."

Counsel for the prosecution sat down, looking well satisfied.

Mr. B. K. Jameson, Q.C., M.P., rose in his turn:

"Dr. Figgins, did you not declare after examining the corpse: 'This is not a child: it's a monkey?' "

"I did."

"Are you still of the same opinion?"

"I am."

"What are your reasons?"

"Certain characteristic traits that were immediately obvious; others that I noticed during the autopsy."

"Such as?"

"The disproportion of the limbs; the foot structure, which is of a frankly simian character, since the thumb is opposed to the other digits; the form of the spine which shows little or no curve in the lumbar region; certain details of the morphology of the face and skull."

"Did you draw the police surgeon's attention to these points?"

"I did."

"Did he agree with your observations?"

"Yes."

"Is it your opinion, therefore, that the prisoner has not caused the death of a human being but of a young animal?"

141

"It is."

Counsel acknowledged this with a word of approval, and sat down. Counsel for the prosecution rose:

"Did not the police surgeon — whom we shall hear presently — conclude in his findings that a murder had been committed on the person of a child?"

"That is so."

"If he had shared your view, would he have come to this conclusion?"

The defense objected to this question.

Counsel for the prosecution resumed:

"Since, in your opinion, the deceased was not a child, would you tell us why you made out a death certificate in the name of Garry Ralph Templemore?"

"As a biologist I may hold that the deceased resembles an ape rather than a man. But this is my personal opinion, and as a general practitioner it is my duty to make out a death certificate for any person whose birth is recorded in the official register and at whose death I am called in."

"Do you recognize by that certificate that whatever doubts you may personally harbor about the nature of the deceased, these do not extend to his legal existence?"

"That is correct."

"In other words, that the deceased was, in law, well ind truly the child of the accused?"

"Yes."

The prosecution sat down. The defense rose and asked:

"Dr. Figgins, do you think that, in this particular case, legal considerations should outweigh zoological ones?"

Counsel for the prosecution objected to the question as soliciting an opinion on the verdict to come.

142

"We shall in that case put the question differently," said counsel. "Dr. Figgins, if the defendant had called you in not at the death of the deceased, but at his birth, would you have agreed, if so requested, to certify him as a human baby?"

"No."

"Not even if the defendant had urged you to?"

"Not even then."

"Does that mean that had it depended on you alone you would have refused the deceased any legal human status?"

"Certainly."

"Just as you would have refused it to a dog or a cat?"

"Just so."

"Is it not a fact, moreover, that you were very reluctant to write out a death certificate, and that you eventually yielded to the defendant's insistence only after he himself had pointed out and proved to you the deceased's legal existence?"

"That is so."

Counsel for the prosecution was about to rise again when the judge stopped him with a gesture and addressed Dr. Figgins:

"To fill some gaps in my zoological knowledge, I should be glad, Dr. Figgins, if you could clarify certain points. The deceased is known to have been the product of a crossbreeding. If, as you seem to think, the issue was an ape, would not at least one of the parents have to be an ape too? Yet I think I remember that one of the criteria of a species, by definition, is that two individuals of different species can between them have no progeny?"

Dr. Figgins coughed and said:

143

"This falls a little outside the sphere of medicine . . . .
However, my lord, I can perhaps enlighten you. A country
doctor is always a bit of a veterinary surgeon as well: he
talks to stockbreeders and is interested in their experiments. Well, my lord, any kind of crossbreeding can be
attempted with a fair chance of success provided the races,
or the species, or even — in very rare cases, it's true —
the genera, are sufficiently close. If it's a cross of strains
or races, the issue is called a half-breed. In the cases of
species or genera, the issue is called a hybrid. Hybridization naturally succeeds less frequently than half-breed-
ing."

"In the case that concerns us here, the deceased was
surely a product of hybridization rather than of half-
breeding?"

"I cannot say so for sure, since I do not know to what
species the female *Paranthropus* belongs."

"Just a moment!" exclaimed the judge. "I no longer
follow you. The child had a man for his father. If his
mother, too, belonged to the human species, how could
the child be an ape?"

"It is perfectly feasible, my lord. Even if the female
Paranthropus proved to be — as I doubt — of human
species, she is in any case of a strain extremely remote
from Occidental man. Now Darwin remarked that in
ducks, for instance, the issue of a cross between two far-
removed domestic strains resembles the wild duck. The
fact is explained by the half-breed's tendency to develop
only those traits common to both parents: and it's obvious
that those common traits can be found only in their common ancestor — that is, the wild creature. In the case

144

before us, the child may have united the simian features common to the *Paranthropus* and to *man* — that is to say, those of some ancient primate."

"So that he may actually be more apelike than either of his parents?"

"Exactly. Or again, something else may have occurred, my lord: there may have been telegony."

"What is that?"

"The influence of an earlier male on a female's later offspring, although he had no share in begetting them. The fact is denied and ridiculed by biologists, but it continues to be generally admitted by breeders. The most famous case is that of Lord Morton's mare. She was first covered by a zebra and produced a half-breed. Then she was served by stallions of the same strain as herself, but continued to breed zebra-marked fillies. If telegony is admitted, then it's not impossible that the female in this case may have been previously fertilized by a male of her own species, or even by some great ape; and the product of the subsequent human fertilization may still bear the marks of it."

"To sum up, then, you think that no definite or even probable conclusion as to the nature, human or otherwise, of the deceased can be drawn from the mere fact that he was engendered by a man?"

"It would, I think, be rash to."

"Would you be prepared, conversely, to testify on oath that the deceased was *not* a human child?"

"On oath? No, my lord. This is merely a personal opinion, I repeat. Others may hold different views on the subject, and be right. Generally speaking, I believe that

145

the matter does not come within the scope of a medical man like myself, but of a specialist in human zoology — that is to say: an anthropologist."

"I see," said the judge. "Thank you, Dr. Figgins."

Dr. Bulbrough, the police surgeon, now entered the witness box. He was very old, with a crown of snow-white hair above a gaunt, earthen-colored face. Age had made him somewhat humpbacked.

"Did Dr. Figgins," counsel for the prosecution began, "draw your attention to the physical constitution of the deceased during the post-mortem examination?"

"He did," said the witness.

"Did you concur with his conclusions?"

"No."

"What were *your* conclusions?"

"That the deceased had met with death as a result of a fatal dose of strychnine chlorhydrate."

"That is not what you were asked," the judge intervened.

"What we want to know," said counsel for the prosecution, "is whether, from your examination, you concluded that the deceased was an ape or a human being?"

"I did not conclude anything at all."

"Why?"

"Because it's neither my job nor my duty to draw conclusions on such points."

"Yet," said counsel for the prosecution, "you did report your findings on the autopsy to the police with a view to prosecution for murder."

"Certainly."

"But no murder can be committed on an ape! So you must have concluded that the deceased was human!"

146

"I concluded nothing. All I have to establish is the immediate physical cause of death, that's all. The rest is the coroner's business. Not mine."

"I've never heard anything like it!" counsel exclaimed.

"There's never *been* anything like it," said the witness.

"You definitely reserve your opinion?"

"I do."

It was impossible to get anything more out of Dr. Bulbrough. The next crown witness was Professor Knaatsch, F.R.A.S. He was a well-known anthropologist whom the Royal College of Natural History, upon consultation by the police, had suggested as an expert able to enlighten the court on the nature of the deceased. He was a wizened, graying, slightly deaf, little man, who constantly ran his hand through his rumpled hair, and spoke in a shrill, hoarse voice. He hardly listened to the question put by the crown before he burst out:

"Poppycock, all of it! What's it you want to know? If those creatures are human? 'Course they're human. They make fire, don't they? They chip stones? They walk upright, don't they? Only look at their astragalus! Ever seen an ape with an astragalus like that? I'm not going to describe it — you wouldn't understand. It's a bone in the ankle. That astragalus alone would be enough. Not to mention the forward range of the tarsus — as long as a finger bone. They've got a monkey's thumb? What of it? We've got an appendix; and a piece in our eardrum that's come down to us from the *Plesiosauris:* what's the use of 'em? They must have lived up in the trees, the tropis, not so far back: fifty or a hundred thousand years ago. But now they've stopped living up there, walk upright, same as us. We all have traits that hark back to

147

the apes! Look at children learning to walk: they still toddle like chimpanzees, on the outer edge of their soles. Look at the big toe of present-day Veddas: articulated so that they can pick up a sixpence from the ground! So they aren't human, ha? Must get clear in your mind what you call human. The Ngandoeng men, what were they? And the Piltdown man, quite close to here? A skull like yours or mine, my lord, with all due respect; but a mandible like a gorilla's. And that other one — which they call Skhul Five, with its small teeth and chin, but a supraorbital ridge as jutting as a gibbon's! Gets you nowhere, all that. The upright posture: that's man. And consequently, the shape of the astragalus, which supports everything: narrow and slender, it's an ape; large and thick, it's a man. There you are. What? What?"

He put his hand to his ear like a trumpet, and turned towards the bench a face racked with nervous twitches.

"I'm talking to the defense!" shouted the judge. "Any questions you wish to put to this witness?"

"No, m'lud," said counsel, "but I wish to make a very unusual request. I should like, with your lordship's permission, one of our witnesses to be called."

The prosecution objected vehemently against this departure from legal custom. The defense pointed out that Professor Knaatsch's opinion could not be contested by laymen, and that the fundamental right of the defense to cross-examine Crown witnesses was thus, in practice, being denied. Since no expert arguments were allowed to counterbalance the impression left in the jury's mind. After some discussion, the judge exceptionally ruled in favor of Counsel's request, and Professor Eatons, F.R.S., Member of the Royal Society of Paleontology and of the

148

Imperial College of Anthropologists, was called. He presented a striking contrast to his predecessor in the witness box: tall, calm, smiling, and extremely distinguished.

"Professor Knaatsch's study of the comparative structure of the anklebones of the chimpanzee, the *Australopithecus*, and a Japanese woman," he began, "is, together with Le Gros Clark's observations on the subject, undoubtedly a classic. But it is to be feared that he has drawn some hasty conclusions. In fact, I regret to have to assure you, my lord, that you have just been listening to a great deal of nonsense. We know quite well that Professor Knaatsch can claim for his view the authority of the great Lamarck, who assumed that man had arboreal, quadrumanous ancestors who gradually became bimanous when they left the forest. But recent indications . . ."

"I don't follow you," the judge interrupted. "Would you mind expressing yourself more simply?"

The jury's flushed, strained faces, their worried, wide-eyed stare, had prompted his request.

"I was explaining," said the witness, "the teaching of Lamarck and his disciples. According to them, as I said, man's forebears used to live in trees, like the apes, and, like them, had four hands to enable them to hang from branches. Then they left the forest, and progressively their lower limbs became modified so that they could walk more easily on the hard ground. And thus there evolved, according to that school of thought, the structure of the human foot as we now know it. Professor Knaatsch still seems to share that opinion. But, unfortunately, recent findings in comparative anatomy hardly support this theory. A general survey of mammals proves, as Frechkop has shown, that the human foot, far from being an ad-

149

vance on that of the ape, is in fact a much more primitive organ, both in plan and design. The ape's foot, even if at first sight this may appear surprising, is clearly of more recent date than ours, which may have come down to us from the Tetrapodes of the Tertiary period. It follows that any creature that is even remotely allied to the tree-dwelling apes by the structure of its foot — as is the case with the tropis — cannot be in the human line of descent."

"Do you mean," asked the judge, "that our foot, such as it is today, already existed in our mammal ancestors, millions of years ago?"

The witness assented.

"And that it improved in the apes, when they began to live in the trees, contrary to Lamarck's assumption that the human foot developed after we had climbed down from the trees?"

"That is so."

"Whence it must be concluded, you think, that the line of descent that ends in man, having always had feet like ours, can never have passed through the ape stage?"

"Exactly."

"And finally, therefore, that the tropis, having an ape's foot, cannot be placed in the line of descent that has always had a human foot?"

"Yes. That's what we call a 'phylum': the tropis cannot be in the phylum which has led to man."

"To put it differently — if I have understood correctly — the tropis would be at the very end of a phylum of apes, rather than at the very start of the human phylum; they are, in your opinion, a strain of particularly highly developed apes and not, as one might believe, a race of still very primitive men?"

150

"That's precisely what I mean. Professor Knaatsch has told us, 'They make fire, they chip stones!' But since the discovery of the *Sinanthropus* we know that an intelligence almost as feeble as the chimpanzee's was capable of such inventions. Moreover, one need only observe the tropis to realize that they seem far more to obey a stimulus than a process of reasoned thought . . . . No," Professor Eatons wound up, "the name of *Paranthropus* that they've been given fits them very well: they are *like* men; but they *aren't* men."

Professor Knaatsch, up in the gallery, was raising his finger and clicking his thumb, to attract Crown counsel's attention.

"Later, later!" said the judge, with a wave of his hand.

"Fantastic!" shouted Professor Knaatsch, in the grip of his wrath, completely deaf to the judge's words and misunderstanding the gesture. He did not even trouble to leave his place — a proceeding unheard of in those surroundings. "Fantastic!" he repeated. "A stimulus! What's a stimulus?"

The judge sternly called him to order, but was unable to make himself heard. Defense counsel motioned with a smile that, for his part, he was prepared to overlook the Professor's absent-mindedness.

"Everything's stimulus!" the old scholar went on, quite unaware of the commotion he was causing. "Even reasoned thought is a stimulus: it comes from something, doesn't it? 'Tisn't Santa Claus, eh? Brain chemistry, all that! Stimulus, intelligence! Nothing but words! One thing alone counts: what you do, what you don't do. The *Sinanthropus?* Well, perhaps he was a man: why not? Show me his astragalus and I'll tell you. By Jove, Profes-

151

sor Eatons, have you forgotten Aristotle? What is it that makes a man? he said. It's the mind; and the mind is the hand. The animals' body, he said, develops into one single specialized tool which they can never change. Whereas the hand becomes claw, pincers, hammer, sword, or any other instrument that prolongs it; hence the need of a mind. And what freed the hand, Professor? The upright posture. On all fours you've no hand, isn't that so? And no hand, no mind. If the astragalus is too weak, you can't stand upright. Therefore what's made the mind? The astragalus. No getting out of it. You disagree, perhaps?"

"I do, if your lordship allows," said Knaatsch's colleague, with a bow of smiling respect to the bench.

"I consider," said the judge thereupon, "that a free discussion is desirable in the interests of this case, since we are dealing not so much with evidence as with an exchange of expert opinions. You may answer, Professor."

Professor Eatons bowed and said:

"The hand created the mind, claims my eminent colleague? I hope he will permit me to hold, indeed, the opposite view. It's not the hand that created the mind, but the mind that created the hand . . . . That seems paradoxical? Why, no, we only have to invert the sequence: the brain, the hand, the erect station. It's because man started to think that he came to stand on his feet so as to free his hands. That is the true meaning of Aristotle: man has hands because he thinks."

"Well," said Knaatsch, "the tropis have hands, haven't they?"

"So have the apes . . . ."

152

"Because they think? And they hold themselves erect, perhaps? Incredible! What balderdash!"

"So have the apes," went on Eatons patiently, "but they have not yet started to use them for intelligent purposes: that is why they have not yet attempted to free their hands by adopting the upright position."

"Then the tropis have started, since they do stand upright? Therefore they're human all right!"

"That isn't enough."

"What more d'you want, then?"

"It wants a whole complex of things, Professor Knaatsch, as you well know. Among the one thousand and sixty-five structural characteristics noted by Keith in man and the different ape species, such as the cranial capacity, number of vertebrae, dental or articular tubercles, and so on, two thirds are common to man and the various apes; all the rest are peculiar to what we call *Homo sapiens*. If but one of those specific traits is lacking — and not only those that apply to the number of neurons of the gray matter and the complexity or subtlety of their connections, but also to the dental formula, the proportion of the sternum parts, of the vertebrae or even of their apophyses — if but a single detail is lacking, we are no longer dealing with man, properly speaking."

"Why, then, Professor, what about Neanderthal man?"

"He was not of the *Homo sapiens* type. We call him man for the sake of convenience."

"What about the Veddas, then, the Pygmies, the Blackfellows, the Bushmen?"

Eatons shrugged his shoulders, spread his hands with a smile of helpless regret.

153

" 'Pon my word, Professor," cried Knaatsch, "you wouldn't by any chance be supporting that infamous article of Julius Drexler's?"

"Drexler's article," said Eatons calmly, "brings a lot of common sense to bear on the subject. It may be that personal conclusions are somewhat hasty and oversimplified. But he is entirely right in safeguarding the integrity and independence of science, and in reminding us that science has no room for sentimental or so-called humanitarian prejudices. The equality of man is no doubt a very worthy aim, but it's not a biologist's business to subscribe to it; except, at most, as my teacher Lancelot Hogben used to say: after eight o'clock at night . . . . And if science were to prove, in the last analysis, that the only genuine man is the white man, if it should appear that the colored races are not absolutely human, we may no doubt find this regrettable; but we must bow to it. And resign ourselves to the fact that antiquity, in using them as slaves, was closer to the truth than we are, who are emancipating them imprudently on the strength of a scientific error. It would therefore be wiser, as Drexler says, to go to the root of the problem, and thus . . ."

A murmur of indignation had welled up from the public gallery, timid at first, then increasingly violent. It finally drowned the voice of Professor Eatons, who ceased speaking though he still maintained his distinguished smile. Mr. Justice Draper glanced at the clock. Almost four-thirty. "Let's turn it to account," he thought. He rose and left the bench. The court was cleared.

154

Chapter 13

SIR Arthur Draper usually took a bus to his club in Pall Mall. It was the Reform Club, from which, one wet morning, Phileas Fogg had set out on his trip round the world. There the judge would quietly read *The Times* until, towards seven, he went home to Onslow Mansions, on the confines of Chelsea and Kensington.

But that evening, the weather being fine and warm, he thought it would be pleasant to take a walk.

The truth was that, perhaps for the first time in thirty years, he did not feel like meeting his old club friends, even if only to read the evening papers in their silent company.

With slow, calm steps he walked along the Embankment and thought of the hearing that had just finished.

155

"What an odd case," he reflected. The judge was well aware of the prisoner's reasons for inviting prosecution. He thought them plucky and pathetic. "But it follows," he thought, "that it is the prosecution which uses against him what must be at bottom his own theory: that the tropis are human. Whereas the defense is compelled to uphold the opposite view and, in order to prove that they are apes, produce witnesses who profess the very type of racial discrimination which the prisoner is risking his life to combat. He has thus had to adopt a line of defense which is in flagrant opposition to the aim he is pursuing . . . . What a tangle! The more so as the Takura Corporation wins the day if it is proved that the tropis are animals . . . . So the prisoner must put all his hopes in the Crown's victory over him . . . . In short, if he wants to win, he must get himself hanged. He can save his life only at the price of defeat . . . . I wonder whether he realized all that, and whether he had thought of it before? Hard to know, since he never says a word."

With the dusk there fell a very light, very blue mist in which the passers-by seemed to merge and mingle in a silent, ghostly ballet. The judge watched them with a fresh curiosity, a new friendliness. "This is mankind," he thought. "Are the tropis part of it? Strange that we can ask the question without the answers coming pat. Strange that, this being so, we must needs conclude that we don't know what marks us out from them . . . . We are forced to face the fact that we never stop to ask ourselves what exactly defines man. We are quite happy just *being* it: there is in the mere fact of being a sort of self-evidence that dispenses with all definitions."

156

A policeman perched on his small island was regulating the traffic with grave, slow solemnity.

"You," thought Sir Arthur, with a touch of tenderness, "you think: 'I'm a policeman. I regulate the traffic.' No doubt it also occurs to you to think: 'I am a British subject.' That again is a clear-cut notion. But how often in the course of your life have you said to yourself: 'I'm a human personality.' It would strike you as preposterous; but isn't that so because, above all, that idea's too vague, because you'd feel, if you were nothing but that, you were floating in mid-air?" The judge smiled: "I'm no different from him," he thought. "I think to myself: 'I'm a judge; I have to give right judgments.' If asked: 'What are you?' I too answer: 'A faithful subject of Her Majesty.' It's so much easier to define an Englishman, a judge, a Quaker, a Labor member, or a policeman, than to define a man pure and simple . . . . The tropis are the living proof of this. And it's infinitely more comfortable to feel you are something which is clear to everyone.

"And here I am," he thought, "all because of those confounded tropis, slipping back into those endless questions that haunt your mind at twenty . . . . Slipping back, or rising to them again?" he mused with sudden candor. "After all, if I've stopped putting them, was it for any very valid reason?" He had been appointed to the bench at an earlier age than is usual in England. He remembered certain problems that troubled his conscience at the time. "By what right do we judge? What is the basis of our judgments? The fundamental concept of guilt — can we even define it? How incredibly presump-

157

tuous to claim to probe another's heart and mind! And absurd, to boot: if mental deficiency lessens a criminal's responsibility, it partly excuses his deed, and we let him off more lightly. Yet why does it excuse his deed? Because he's less able than others to resist his impulses; but for that very reason he will relapse. He therefore, more than others, ought to be rendered harmless, sentenced more harshly, more lastingly, than the man who has no excuse: for the latter will afterwards find the strength to control himself in his reasoning power and in the memory of his punishment. Yet an inner feeling tells us that this would be neither fair, nor humane. Thus justice and public welfare are implacably opposed to one another." He remembered that these dilemmas had troubled him so deeply that he had thought of resigning his office. And then, little by little, he had become hardened. Less than others. The incredible sclerosis of most of his colleagues caused him constant surprise and dismay. Still, he had eventually told himself, like the others, that it was fruitless to waste time and energy on insoluble problems. Had put his trust, with belated wisdom, in rules, in traditions, in legal precedent. Had even come to despise, from the lofty vantage point of age, the presumptuous young whippersnapper who had claimed to set his puny individual conscience against the whole edifice of British justice! . . .

But here he was, at the end of his life, faced with a baffling problem, which suddenly, brutally, challenged everything again, since neither rules nor tradition nor legal precedents could provide an answer. And he honestly could not say whether he was vexed or delighted.

A ripple of silent, anarchic, disrespectful laughter that welled up within him at these thoughts told him that delight was the uppermost feeling. For one thing, it admirably suited his inveterate sense of humor. And then, he loved his youth. He loved it and exulted at having to pronounce in its favor.

With gleeful apostasy he now reviewed those rules, those precedents, that whole baggage of venerable traditions, reviewed them with a ruthlessly critical eye. "At bottom," he thought, "we live on taboos, like the savages. Thou shalt, thou shalt not. Our commands, our prohibitions are never founded on an irreducible bedrock. For all things human can, like chemical compounds, always be further and further reduced to other human components, short of ever reaching the one simple element: a definition of what is 'human.' That's the one thing we've never defined. It's really unbelievable! Now what are unfounded prohibitions, if not taboos? Savages believe in the sanction and necessity of their taboos just as stoutly as we do in ours. The only difference is that ours are a lot more elaborate. We no longer seek their causes in magic or totems, but in religion or philosophy; in our day we seek them in history and sociology. It also happens that we invent new taboos. Or swap them — though rarely — in mid-stream. Or modify them, in spite of tradition, when they have become too patently harmful or out of date. I readily admit that, on the whole, they are fine, splendid taboos. Useful too, no doubt. Quite indispensable to social life. But in the light of what, then, do we judge social life? Not just its present form, or the form it may assume: but whether it is a good thing in itself; or merely necessary to something outside itself: to whom? to what? That too is a taboo, nothing more."

He stopped at the curb, waiting till the crossing should be clear.

"We Christians," he mused, "have the Word, the Revelation: 'Love your neighbor as yourself. Turn the other cheek.' Now that is utterly opposed to the great natural laws. That's why we consider that the Word is beautiful. But why do we consider that it is beautiful to oppose nature? Why must we, on that point, break with the laws that all animals obey? 'The will of God' is no doubt a sufficient answer to constrain us, but not to explain this constraint. If these aren't taboos, I'll be hanged!"

He stepped off the curb to cross the road by Westminster Bridge.

"If I said all this aloud, people would think I was blaspheming. Yet I'm not in the least conscious of blaspheming. For I deeply hold that, taboo or no taboo, the Word is good. Perhaps just because it breaks with Nature, with her universal law of 'eat or be eaten'? So justice, charity, all the taboos in short, would be anti-Nature? . . . If you think it over, it seems obvious enough: for why have laws, rules, commandments, why have morals or virtue, if it isn't because we have to dam in and defeat Nature's powerful promptings to our weakness . . . . Yes, yes, all our taboos are founded on anti-Nature. Well, well," he suddenly said to himself, with a thrill of exhilaration, "mightn't that be an irreducible basis? Isn't that a glimmer of light?"

He had begun to think: "The question is, perhaps:

160

have the tropis any taboos?" when the sound of wheels
screeching under the sudden impact of brakes threw him
back with a start. In the nick of time! He remained for
a while on the traffic island, with throbbing heart. He
could not afterward pick up the thread of his thoughts.

A little later he was sitting down to dinner in the cold
dining room of Onslow Mansions. Lady Draper faced
him at the other end of the dark polished mahogany
table. They were silent, as was their custom. Sir Arthur
was very fond of his wife, who was affectionate, devoted,
brave and faithful, and, moreover, of excellent family.
But he considered her to be exquisitely foolish and un-
tutored in mind, as was only proper in a respectable
household. Thus she never asked unseemly questions
about his professional life. Nor did she appear to have
much to say for herself. All this favored mental relaxation.

That evening, however, she suddenly said:

"I very much hope you will not sentence that young
Templemore. It would be a very wicked thing to do."

Sir Arthur turned a surprised and slightly shocked gaze
on his wife.

"But dearest, that's neither your nor my affair. The
decision rests entirely with the jury."

"Oh," said Lady Draper sweetly, "you know quite
well that the jury will follow your lead, if you wish it."

She poured a little mint sauce over her boiled leg
of mutton.

"I should be vexed on account of little Frances," she
said. "Her mother was an old and dear friend of my
elder sister's."

161

"That," began Sir Arthur, "could not in any way influence . . ."

"Of course not," said his wife quickly. "Still," she added, "she's a charming girl. Wouldn't it be horribly unfair to kill her husband?"

"Doubtless, but after all . . . the administration of British justice cannot possibly take into account . . ."

"I sometimes wonder," said Lady Draper, "if what you call justice . . . I mean, when justice isn't just, I wonder . . . Does that never bother you?" she questioned.

This incredible intrusion of his wife into the very crux of his profession left Sir Arthur so dumfounded that he could not at first find an answer.

"Besides," she continued a little later, "by what right would you send him to the gallows?"

"But, my dear . . ."

"You know quite well that, after all, he's merely killed a little animal."

"Nobody yet knows . . ."

"Oh come, everything goes to show it."

"What do you call 'everything'?"

"Oh, how should *I* know? It's perfectly obvious," she said, daintily raising her fork, on which a blob of pink blancmange was quivering.

"What is perfectly obvious? Really, you —"

"How should I know?" she said again. "For instance, look: they don't even have *ju-jus*."

"They don't have what?"

"*Ju-jus.* Charms, you know."

Sir Arthur was later to remember this remark and how much it may have influenced the course of the trial: for

162

it linked up with his own question, which it now recalled to his mind: "Have the tropis any taboos?"

But at the moment he was alive only to the ludicrous side of it.

"*Ju-jus!*" he cried. "Why, do *you* wear *ju-jus?*"

She shrugged her shoulders and smiled.

"Sometimes I'm not so sure. Not so sure that I don't have them, I mean. Or that your lovely wig in court is not a *ju-ju* too."

She raised her hand to forestall his objection. It pleased him to notice, once again, what a distinguished, white and still beautiful hand it was.

"I am not pulling your leg," she said. "Everybody has the *ju-jus* suitable to his age, I think. Peoples, too, no doubt. The youngest have the simplest ones. The others need more complicated *ju-jus*. But all have them, I think. Yet, don't you see, the tropis haven't any."

Sir Arthur remained silent. He was gazing at his wife in astonishment. She went on, while folding her napkin:

"You do need *ju-jus*, don't you, once you believe in something? If you believe in nothing . . . I mean, you can of course refuse to believe in the accepted things, that does not prevent . . . Even those bright people, I mean, who pretend they don't believe in anything, we see them seeking for something, don't we? They study . . . physics or . . . astronomy, or else write books: these are their *ju-jus*, of a sort. It's their way of . . . of defending themselves . . . against all those things that make us so afraid when we think of them . . . . Don't you agree?"

He nodded silently. She was twisting her napkin in its silver-gilt ring with an absent-minded gesture.

163

"But if people *really* don't believe in anything," she said, ". . . if they have no *ju-jus* at all . . . then they have never asked themselves any questions, have they? Once you start asking yourself . . . it seems to me . . . you can't help being afraid. And once you are afraid . . . . Look, Arthur, even those poor primitive Negroes we saw in Ceylon, you remember, the ones who were so awfully backward they didn't know how to do anything, not even count up to five, hardly speak . . . they still had *ju-jus*. So they must have believed in something. And if they believe . . . well, then, they must have wondered what there is in the sky, or somewhere . . . in the forest . . . I don't know . . . well, things they could believe in . . . . Do you see? Even those poor brutes have wondered about it. So if a creature doesn't ask itself any questions . . . just absolutely nothing, nothing at all . . . well, I think it really must be a beast. If you are not a complete beast, I imagine you can't live and act on this earth without ever asking yourself anything at all. Don't you think so? Even a village idiot asks himself things . . ."

They had risen. Sir Arthur walked over to his wife and put his arm around her in a temperate embrace. He dropped a discreet kiss on her ear.

"You have said some strange things, my dear. They'll make me do some thinking, I believe. In fact, I'd like to do it at once, if you don't mind. Before that visitor turns up."

Lady Draper gently brushed her gray hair against her husband's.

"You'll get him acquitted, won't you?" she said with a bland smile. "I should be so grieved for that poor girl."

164

"Once again, dearest, the jury alone . . . "

"But you will do your best?"

"You're not asking me to promise anything, I suppose?" said Sir Arthur mildly.

"Certainly not. I trust in your fairness, Arthur."

They kissed each other again, and he went into his study and buried himself at once in a deep armchair.

"The tropis have no taboos," he said, almost aloud. "They do not draw, they do not sing, they have no feasts or rites, no signs, no witchcraft, they have no *ju-jus*. They are not even cannibals."

In an even louder voice he said:

"Can there be men without taboos?"

Absent-mindedly he gazed before him at the portrait of Sir Weston Draper, Baronet, Knight of the Garter. He was aware of a sort of inner smile that slowly rose to his lips.

Chapter 14

PROFESSOR RAMPOLE'S STATEMENT AND CAPTAIN
THROPP'S REFUTATION. FINAL TESTIMONIES AND
CLOSING SPEECHES FOR THE PROSECUTION AND
FOR THE DEFENSE. MR. JUSTICE DRAPER'S SUM-
MING-UP. THE JURY'S PERPLEXITY. NEED OF A
PRIOR DEFINITION OF MAN IN ORDER TO DEFINE
THE TROPI. THE INCREDIBLE LACK OF SUCH A
DEFINITION IN THE CODES OF LAW. THE JURY
REFUSES TO PRONOUNCE THEMSELVES.

A T the next hearing, the Crown called two more anthropologists as its last witnesses. But though they were
agreed in classifying the *Paranthropus* in the human
species, they proved so profoundly divided on the zoological reasons for their opinion that the defense merely
withdrew into an ironic silence, more eloquent than any
argument.

After Counsel had opened the case for the defense,
he called two psychologists: Professor Rampole, an authority on the psychology of primitive races, and Captain

Thropp, widely renowned for his studies on the intelligence of the great apes.

Professor Rampole was wondrously bald, as if he had wished to offer the perfect skull to students of phrenology. A monocle was clamped into his — practically blind — right eye, which made him look rather like a former officer in the Imperial German Army. But a warm, sensitive, musical voice soon made you forget his peculiar appearance.

The first question put to him seemed to embarrass him not a little: is there any recognizable trait by which the most primitive human intelligence differs specifically, intrinsically, from animal intelligence?

Sir Peter said after a moment that a few months ago he would still have replied: the language. Human language is articulate, the animal's is not. The former bears the mark of invention and memory, the latter is fixed and instinctive. But since then the tropis had appeared, and their language, though apparently instinctive, was yet articulate; there was nothing to prove that it was fixed and devoid of invention, since it had shown itself capable of growth — but so far only by imitation. Their language was thus akin to both types without being either. All this had forced him to admit that he had not pushed his conclusions far enough: he now realized that since language was only a means of communication, the truly specific traits resided in the inner urge to communicate — and in the sort of things a creature wanted to communicate.

He paused to ponder, then added:

"Some people think that this specific difference must

be sought in man's myth-creating propensity. Others, in his use of symbols — first and foremost: words. But in both cases we soon find ourselves facing the same problem as before: what is the specific urge to which the creation of myths or symbols responds?"

He passed his large, gnarled hand over his gleaming skull.

"I don't think, you know, that we can get very far in this direction. It is safer to keep to facts that can be verified: those that are brought to light by an analysis of the various brain connections. A comparative study of those connections in man and beast might possibly yield a positive, clear-cut distinction."

"I am not quite sure I follow you," remarked the judge.

"The brain has often been likened to a vast telephone exchange," said Sir Peter. "With incredible speed it connects thousands of offices, some engaged in observation or study, the others in charge of management or control. On the whole, these connections have been ascertained with considerable precision. What I mean is that we know fairly accurately their number and respective function in man and the different animal species. I think therefore it would be proper to call 'human' any being whose brain contains all these connections, and 'animal' any creature whose brain does not."

"For the number of these connections," Mr. Justice Draper elaborated, "is identical in all human beings, whatever their age, intelligence or race?"

"N . . . no," said Sir Peter, rubbing the side of his nose. "That would be too easy. There are differences, even great ones. . . . Still . . . that need not trouble us unduly. For in actual fact the mass of connections displayed by

168

the most backward Negrillo is still incomparably more complete than those of the most intelligent chimpanzee. Let us put it this way, if you like: the brain connections of a Negrillo represent both in quality and quantity the minimum below which a creature is not entitled to the name of human being."

The judge nodded thoughtfully for a few seconds before suggesting:

"Mightn't that — as a basis of classification — be a little too arbitrary, not to say: specious? For it boils down, doesn't it, to taking, first, the brain connections of the Negrillo as the lowest human minimum, and then declaring, as a result, that the Negrillos are undoubtedly human since they do indeed have those connections?"

The professor laughed good-humoredly, and said:

"That's true, my lord. But I don't quite see how we can avoid that vicious circle."

"On the other hand," said the judge, "are you not contradicting yourself? If certain connections are missing, you say, a creature is not human. Now does this lack correspond to an absence of certain traits of intelligence?"

"Yes, indeed."

"So doesn't that amount to saying that one ceases to be human if those traits of intelligence are lacking? Yet that assertion you claimed, a moment ago, to be, if not impossible, at least extremely rash."

"You're perfectly right," admitted the professor.

"Must we conclude then," asked the judge, "that psychology is as little able as zoology to locate the exact borderline between . . . beast and man?"

Mr. Justice Draper turned to Counsel for the defense:

169

"I should like to put a few further questions to this witness, for the sake of clarification, but perhaps you would like to proceed with your examination of him first?"

"Clarification is indeed my aim, my lord. If your lordship wishes to question Professor Rampole, I am quite content."

"Thank you, Mr. Jameson," said the judge and, after covertly smiling in the direction of a a pink-and-pale-green tulle hat at the back of the court, he asked:

"Professor, I understand that there is no tribe on the face of the globe, on the farthermost island, or in the heart of the deepest jungle, whose psychology you have not studied in all its aspects. Have you ever met a tribe that had no *ju-jus?*"

A smile swept through the public, welcome as a respite, as a rest. But the professor did not smile. He hardly hesitated before replying:

"No, indeed. Never."

"To what do you ascribe the constancy of this feature?"

"What exactly do you want to know, my lord?"

"Whether this constancy in time and space might not denote a specifically human trait?"

"Yes. Like the myth-creating faculty. It does not get us much further."

"I'm not so sure," said the judge. "Is it not a faculty, an inclination, peculiar to man and man alone, to ask himself questions — even the simplest, the most elementary ones?"

"No doubt."

"Can one not," continued the judge, "ascribe this

170

faculty to certain brain connections that do not exist in the animal?"

"Can one?" repeated Professor Rampole thoughtfully. "Curiosity exists in animals too. Many animals are exceedingly curious."

"But they do not have *ju-jus?*" asked the judge.

"No."

"So it isn't the same kind of curiosity. They haven't asked the same questions."

"That is true," said Sir Peter. "The metaphysical mind is peculiar to man. The animal doesn't have it."

"Can one be quite sure of it, though? Has no animal ever shown signs of that type of curiosity, even at its most rudimentary level?"

"I don't think so," said Sir Peter. "This is rather outside my sphere, but on the face of it . . . The animal watches, observes, waits to see what this or that thing will do, or become, but . . . that's all. If the object disappears, his curiosity disappears with it. Never this . . . this refusal, this struggle against the silence of things. For the fact is that the animal's curiosity has remained purely functional: it does not really apply to the thing as such, but only to its relationship with himself; the animal always remains part of things — part of nature, in every fiber. He never detaches himself from things in order to know or understand them from outside. In a word," concluded Sir Peter, "the animal is incapable of abstract thinking. There indeed we may have . . . a network of connections . . . a specific network given to man, and man alone."

Nobody having any more questions to put, the judge

171

thanked the professor and allowed him to stand down.

Captain Thropp, pink, chubby, very fair, with lively, laughing eyes, followed him in the witness box. Counsel reminded the jury that Captain Thropp had read several scientific papers to the Natural History Society on his studies and tests on great apes, and that his reputation had long ago spread beyond the British Isles.

He briefly summed up for Captain Thropp's benefit the statement made by Professor Rampole and the discussion that had followed it. Then he asked:

"Do you consider, Captain Thropp, that the most intelligent of the great apes are utterly incapable of abstract thinking?"

"Why, not at all!" said the little man.

"I beg your pardon?" inquired the judge.

"They are perfectly capable of it, my lord. Just like you and me."

The judge's eyelids flicked. There was a pause.

"Professor Rampole told us . . ." the judge at last began.

"I know, I know," broke in Captain Thropp. "All these people take animals for nitwits!"

Mr. Justice Draper could not repress a smile, and everyone in court relaxed and smiled with him.

"You haven't read my paper," Captain Thropp went on, "on Wolfe's experiments? Well, he gave his chimpanzees a slot machine: you put in counters, and out come raisins. The chimps quickly got the hang of it. Then he gave them another slot machine that produced the counters. The chimps made it work, then promptly took the counters to the first machine. This he then locked. Thereupon the apes hid their counters, hoarding

172

them for the day when he'd come and unlock the machine again. They had reinvented money, and even avarice! Not abstract thinking, that? And Verlaine! Not the French poet — the Belgian professor. His tests on a macaco. A *lower* monkey, mind you! Well, he proved that this monkey could perfectly well tell living from dead matter, distinguish between animal, vegetable, mineral kingdoms, between metal, wood, fabric; never made a mistake, not even when it came to bird's down and cotton flock, a nail and a matchstick, each sorted according to its kingdom. Not abstract thinking, that? And as for speech! It is generally thought that monkeys can't talk. But they jolly well can! Sixty years ago Garner established that there's merely a quantitative difference between our language and theirs: we even have a number of sounds in common with the monkeys. I know that Delage and Boutan, in France, have refuted it. But it's a fact that Giacomini, in his comparative study of the anatomy of the larynx, has shown the rising scale of perfection to be as follows: orangoutang, gorilla, gibbon, chimpanzee, male Bushman, female Negro, male white man. Why shouldn't the gradation of speech be parallel? We don't understand the monkey's talk? Is that their fault? In point of fact, my lord, they're a sight cleverer at understanding ours. Gladden had a chimpanzee who responded without hesitation to forty-three commands unaccompanied by any gestures. Isn't that abstract thinking? And Furness managed to teach a young orang the word 'papa.' This was difficult because an animal tends to swallow the sound it's being taught rather than to breathe it out. But anyway, once he could say 'papa,' he used the word for any male person that came near, but never for a woman. That no abstract thinking? Then Furness taught him the word 'cup,' by placing a spatula on his tongue. Sounds artificial, but from then on the orang said 'cup' every time he was thirsty. Not abstract thinking, huh? At last Furness tried to teach him the article 'the'; now that's a pure abstraction. Unfortunately the young animal died before he'd succeeded."

"That doesn't surprise me very much," remarked Justice Draper. "I have many French friends who, though reasonably intelligent, have never learned to pronounce that word properly, either. Poor little monkey . . . . However," he continued, "perhaps I did not frame the question as I should have done. What we actually want to know is whether you — or anyone else to your knowledge — have ever noticed in a monkey the rudiments of a metaphysical turn of mind?"

"Metaphysical turn of mind . . ." repeated Captain Thropp, and drooping his head in deep absorption, he now had a treble chin. "What do you mean by that?" he asked finally.

"By that I mean . . . an inner disquiet," said the judge, "the fear of the unknown, the desire for an explanation, the capacity to believe in something . . . . In other words, have you ever known a monkey to have *ju-jus?*"

"I have known some," said the captain, "who loved things in the way a baby loves its Teddy bear: they played and slept with them. But they weren't *ju-jus.* In another order of ideas, I once knew a young she-monkey in Calcutta who had an inveterate sense of decency: she never went to sleep without first carefully

174

concealing what is seemly with a green slipper which she would never be parted from. But *ju-jus?* No. And anyway," he burst out suddenly, "why the dickens do you want them to have *ju-jus?* They live with nature, right inside nature, they aren't afraid of it! It's all right for savages to be afraid! All right for them to ask themselves idiotic questions! Where does it get 'em? If they can't be content, like monkeys, to be as they are, as God made 'em, it's nothing to be proud of! Anarchists of a sort, that's what they are! A pack of rebels, never content. Why do you want my good chimps to ask themselves stupid questions? *Ju-jus,* indeed! You can keep 'em, thank you kindly!"

"I assure you," Sir Arthur told him with twinkling good humor, "that I don't want anything at all. Except to be certain of your reply: no trace of a metaphysical mind, or anything approaching it, in any ape?"

"Not the slightest! Not the tiniest iota of a trace! Not *that* much!" said the other triumphantly, snapping his finger against his thumb.

"And you, Captain Thropp," asked the defense suavely, "don't you ask yourself any questions either?"

"What questions?" retorted Captain Thropp in astonishment. "I'm a good Christian. I believe in God and all the rest of it. Why d'you want me to . . . Do you take me for a savage?"

Sir Arthur amiably assured him of the contrary and thanked him, and the captain left the witness box. Then Greame, Williams, Kreps, and Father Dillighan were called in turn to relate in detail their observations on the tropis and the tests they had carried out. Few ques-

175

tions were put to them. Counsel for the defense showed more clearly than ever that he was not out to gain an advantage or score a point, but only to keep restoring an exact balance, that is to say: the most perfect indecision. Whenever the Crown stressed a point that seemed to argue in favor of the tropis' humanity, the defense put some question that would elicit a contradictory fact or observation. If, on the other hand, a witness produced arguments that might seem too solidly to support the animal nature of the tropis, the defense went out of its way to raise some other point, this time designed to bring out their human side. Whereupon the Crown triumphantly shook its sleeves, and the jurymen could no longer make head or tail of Counsel's peculiar line of defense.

Father Dillighan was the last witness to be heard. The liveliness and drollery of his testimony relaxed everybody's mind. For he mainly dealt with the tropi language, and uttered a number of imitative cries. The public would have liked to applaud, and when he withdrew he was pounced upon by a tenacious old lady who insisted on telling him all about her parrots, and refused to be shaken off.

ᕼᕦᕤ

Sir Carew W. Minchett, counsel for the prosecution, crossed his long white hands. He silently bowed his head, as if about to pray, thus offering to the jury's contemplation the impeccable curls of his fine white wig. Then, raising his head, he said:

"Ladies and gentlemen of the jury, I can imagine your perplexity.

"That the prisoner has deliberately killed the deceased,

176

that of course is beyond any doubt. My learned friend himself, we may be sure, will not attempt to deny it.

"But my learned friend has made every effort to raise a doubt in your mind as to the nature of the deceased, in order to secure the prisoner's acquittal on the strength of one of our most cherished, time-honored traditions — that of giving an accused man the benefit of every reasonable doubt.

"We are therefore compelled to ask ourselves whether there does exist a reasonable doubt as to the nature of the victim. I suggest that if such doubt appears to exist, it is only an illusion.

"The truth is that my learned friend has succeeded in confusing the issue by conducting his case on two completely different planes which are clearly distinct but which he has most cunningly confounded: the legal, judicial plane, and the zoological one.

"What, however, ladies and gentlemen of the jury, is your business in this court? Is it to judge facts, or to arbitrate between experts?

"Distinguished professors and men of science have been called to argue before you. You were able to see for yourselves that they agreed on nothing, not even on what is a man. Is it your task to teach them their business? To tell them which of them is right?

"You may of course object: 'Didn't you yourself raise the issue by calling Professor Knaatsch as a witness?' That is true enough: but it was easy to foresee that the defense would call experts to uphold the views you have since heard. They had to be contradicted lest you be misled into believing them.

"Now what is the upshot of all those arguments? As

177

far as you are concerned, it is this in a nutshell: that you are asked to know more than those eminent scholars! Is that what you have been called here for? And if it isn't, if you cannot be expected to know more than they do, is that a reason for claiming that *the facts* are in doubt? Simply because you have been artfully befogged by arguments too complicated for you to follow?

"No, you are not here to form an opinion on the merits or demerits of this or that zoological classification; nor to declare whether the school that calls *Paranthropus* what another calls *Homo faber* is right or wrong. You are here to judge of facts on a legal and judicial basis.

"Now, on that basis, is there the slightest room for doubt?

"Can you entertain any doubt that the prisoner deliberately put to death a child born to him, a child whom he himself had had baptized and entered in the register of births under the name of Garry Ralph Templemore?

"No, you cannot doubt it.

"Perhaps, however, some last doubt does nevertheless linger in your minds. The doubt whether it is not in any case preferable to acquit a man who is of a certainty a criminal rather than to convict one who may just possibly be innocent? And that any uncertainty, even that arising from the academic disputes you have heard, commands you in fact to let the prisoner have the benefit of it, be he a thousand times guilty?

"Yes, that might be admitted as an act of Christian charity, if the prisoner alone were on trial here. If the only risk attendant on your leniency were that of letting one murderer off scot-free.

178

"But is that the case? Do you think that there stands but one accused before you in this court? No, do not believe it: it only appears so. There are a thousand, there are ten thousand, there are perhaps ten million accused in the dock!

"Ah, ladies and gentlemen of the jury, your responsibility is heavy indeed. Never perhaps, in all my career, have I known a heavier one. For your verdict may have future consequences that transcend not only the prisoner's person, but yours, and mine, and even the whole institution of British justice.

"For imagine for a moment that, yielding to the exhortations with which my learned friend will not fail to overwhelm you, you let your heart and your compassion speak too loudly; that, wishing to act fairly according to your lights, you deem it your duty to consider whether the prisoner, in murdering his child, did not sincerely believe he was killing an ape; in short that, wishing him to be acquitted, you return a verdict of not guilty! That verdict, whether you wish it or not, will be tantamount to a public declaration that the victim *was an ape*. That — at any rate — is the interpretation that will be put on it, irrevocably, by your fellow citizens, and by those many more millions abroad who are watching and waiting for your decision. It also follows that you will, by a single word, have excluded — perhaps forever — all tropis from the human community. And not only the tropis, but countless human groups, since many an eminent person here has shown you that if it is admitted that the tropis are animals, it will later be hard indeed to find a sound basis for asserting that the Pygmies or the Bushmen are

179

really men. Do you realize what a baneful Pandora's box you are in danger of opening? For if those primitive tribes were one day to be outstripped of their human status and, consequently, of human rights, it would be you who would have delivered them up defenselessly, into the hands of those who are out to destroy or exploit them and whom *you* will have empowered to do so with impunity. And we know, unfortunately, that they are legion.

"Nor would it stop there. For it has also been shown you that if, on the strength of biological differences, the sacred oneness of the human species is called in doubt, there will be no barriers left at which to cry halt! And but one of the lesser horrors would be, I fear, the revival of those criminal racial hierarchies which we still have in odious memory. And it would be you who had unleashed this new disaster. This is a prospect that may well strike fear into the hearts even of those more learned than you. The law, I repeat, does not ask you to be learned. It asks you to apply your common sense. This involves neither risk nor effort. All you have to do is to consider this case from the only viewpoint that concerns this court. This, as we have seen, is the viewpoint of the law. Douglas Templemore has killed Garry Ralph Templemore, his son. That is enough. You can but find him guilty."

Sir Carew W. Minchett crossed once more the fingers of his long, white hands.

"He is guilty," he added, "not only of a murder, but of a fully premeditated one. It may be that the prisoner, in acting as he did, had some aim in mind which he believed of benefit to mankind. But do not forget that those loathsome doctors in the camps of death also claimed that the heinous experiments they had perpetrated were of great profit to human knowledge! Thus, your leniency now would be not only an unpardonable display of levity liable to expose your fellow countrymen to further crimes, and many an innocent people to slavery and death, but it would also open the way to monstrous and murderous experiments in the future, under the fallacious pretext of serving science and progress. And finally it would, at best, be an insult to the prisoner himself. For in wishing to render him his life and liberty, which he knowingly sacrificed in committing his act, you would deprive that very act of the only aspect which allows it to retain a dubious dignity.

"Ladies and gentlemen of the jury, I will say no more. Why expatiate further on so clear a case? Let my learned friend choose to speak at length since he must seek to prove the unprovable: that the prisoner did not kill his son. He killed him. These three words are enough to convict him."

Sir Carew W. Minchett had finished. He sat down.

The judge turned to the defense.

Mr. B. K. Jameson rose to say:

"In conformity with the wishes of the defendant, I shall not plead for him in a final speech."

However, he did not resume his seat, and as if unaware of the murmer of surprise which the public could not suppress, he went on:

"I must even declare that I am on more than one point in full agreement with my learned friend. Especially when he extorts you to bear in mind the grave responsibility

181

that rests upon you. Weigh well the consequences of a mistake, he said. But I do not draw the same inferences as he does. Oh no, ladies and gentlemen of the jury, do not as he suggests, lazily keep to the trodden path not of law, but of mere legal formalism: of red tape, in fact! An entry in a register! Suppose that an undergraduate, in misguided high spirits, plays a hoax on the registrar by having his puppy's birth entered as if it were a child's. And suppose again that, years later, when the dog has grown lame and old, it is put to sleep by a veterinary surgeon. The next thing you know the vet's up for murder, and my learned friend wants him dispatched to the gallows!

"The suggestion is ludicrous. But the other arguments advanced by the prosecution are more serious. He has asked you to beware of the consequences of an acquittal which would presume *ipso facto* that the tropis are apes. This is a grave consideration. But what if the tropis really *are* apes? Would it be less grave in your eyes to send a man to the gallows, were it to avenge a thousand apes? Knowingly to send to his death an innocent man, to perpetrate — as you are asked to do — so grave an injustice, simply to spare yourselves the trouble of hard thinking! What name would you give to such conduct? It is a crime against a man of high merit, as well as an offense against our most sacred rights. For if the freedom, the life, of an Englishman came to depend not on what he has done but on the hypothetical results of his acquittal, then we should all of us be delivered over, bound and gagged, to the blind caprice of the powers that be. Which of us could be sure of the morrow? It would be tanta-

182

mount to deciding, in one breath, that the individual does not count. It would mean the death of our liberties.

"No, ladies and gentlemen, you cannot find the prisoner guilty unless you are certain, absolutely certain, that he has killed a human being — or, in general terms, that the tropis are human. Even at the risk of surprising my learned friend, I shall not try to prove the contrary. For what we are defending here is not one individual's right to justice. We are defending truth. We shall not prove that the tropis are apes, for had the defendant been sure of that, he would not have put to death an innocent little creature and offered his own neck to the infamy of the hangman's noose. He still does so unflinchingly. But if his life be forfeit, let it serve at least to reveal the one thing that matters: not a vague preference or expediency, but justice and truth — and let them stand revealed not in a dubious half-light, but in the bright blaze of day. Yes, the accused is willing to have his life sacrificed for the tropis if it may thereby be proved beyond a doubt that they are human, thus forcing those who plan to enslave them to desist from their schemes. But if the tropis are apes, then I declare it would be infamous to convict a man for the incredible reason that it is simply more convenient!

"Our position is clear. Yours must be no less so. We do not want mercy or pardon. We refuse your leniency. Yes, let it be well understood: we *refuse* it. But I ask of you the least to which the accused is entitled: your most earnest reflection."

Mr. Jameson, to indicate that he had finished, sat down and lightly patted his curls.

183

Mr. Justice Draper looked at the clock. A quarter to four. He glanced at the members of the jury. They too were looking at the clock. Their strained faces seemed to revive at the idea that they could at last relax that exhausting attention, rest their minds till the next day, and collect their wits. Already the jurors were fidgeting like a class of expectant schoolboys waiting for the bell that will sound their release. Then they saw the judge was sternly gazing at them, and they stopped still.

"Counsel for the Defense has been brief," said the judge. "I thank him for it. It enables me to pass at once to the summing up, and if you, members of the jury, will make the necessary effort, you may be able to return your verdict tonight, thus saving us all another day's hearing."

The poor jury, sitting there motionless, presented a woeful sight. The judge seemed not to notice it. Below him, on the barristers' bench, the Crown and the defense, their wigged heads put together, were talking in animated whispers. Mr. Jameson rose and said with some feeling:

"With your Lordship's permission, it seems to me . . . and my learned friend agrees with me on this point . . . that if the jury have to . . . if they lack the necessary time, not only to rest their minds, clear them of all confusion and put their thoughts in order, but also to deliberate in the unhurried tranquillity indispensable to so serious a —"

"The jury," the judge cut him short, "will have all the time they want. They can deliberate for three days or even a week, if they wish. But I see no reason why they should not make the small effort today to try and avoid

184

another day's hearing." And having spoken thus, the judge put on his glasses.

‹◦›

There was a long, rather heavy silence. In the crowded gallery could be heard the shuffle of feet and some suppressed coughing. There was an outbreak of whispering on the right, but a hundred heads turning in disapproval quickly nipped it in the bud.

Douglas was looking at Sir Arthur. Since the beginning of the trial Douglas had forced himself never to glance in Frances's direction. He had striven to be mute, impassive, almost absent. It was an arduous part to play, and one that tortured the nerves. Had he caught but one glance from Frances — sad, frightened or imploring — could he have stood the strain? It was agony, too, never to turn his eyes towards that lovely, stricken face with the wide mouth . . . . But between two tortures, he must at least choose the one that gave some purpose to the risk he had accepted. He had not succeeded too badly up to now.

Frances was not under the same compulsion to control herself. Sitting between Greame and Sybil, she seemed to hang on each word with her eyes as much as with her ears. Sometimes she gripped Sybil's wrist almost hard enough to break it. Sometimes she leaned back, as if exhausted, closing her eyes. When the judge refused counsel's request, Frances had to bite her lips till they bled, to maintain a semblance of calm. But her heart was suddenly drained.

Douglas had not moved a muscle. Oh, how she wanted

185

him to look at her, just once, just this once! But they had
promised each other that he would not do it, that she
would not even wish him to. He was right, he was right!
And she turned her head away.

Now she too was looking at the judge. Sir Arthur was
slowly putting on his glasses. And then, at the very
moment that he settled them on the bridge of his nose,
she caught quite plainly . . . yes, a strange little wink,
laughing, furtive, friendly, almost conspiratorial, which
he slipped, in the flicker of an eyelid, towards the accused.

"Did you see?" she whispered excitedly into Sybil's ear.

"Yes," said Sybil, "yes . . . you'd almost say he . . ."

She did not finish, and Frances saw with amazement
that she was touching the wood of the seat three times.

"You didn't know I was superstitious?" grinned Sybil.

"I certainly didn't," said Frances. "If anybody ever
seemed to me . . ."

"You still don't know the half about me . . . . But look
at Douglas!"

Douglas seemed petrified. But if he had been turned to
marble, it was pink marble. He had gone pink to the roots
of his hair. His lips were half open, his eyes goggling. He
was staring at the judge as if he were the Angel of the
Annunciation.

"He saw it too!" murmured Frances. "Please God that
. . ."

But Sybil pressed her arm to stop her, to avert the evil
eye. Besides, Mr. Justice Draper was beginning to speak.

"Ladies and gentlemen of the jury," he said. "During
the last three days you have heard the witnesses for the

Crown and for the defense, you have heard the closing speech for the prosecution, and the accused has wished to spare you a final plea in his defense. You now have to decide on the prisoner's fate. But before you do so, it is my duty briefly to sum up for you the facts of the case in order to help you, if possible, to reach this grave and difficult decision.

"For it is indeed both grave and difficult. Yours is a formidable task; both sides have impressed this fact upon you. I shall not therefore enlarge upon that point. But I must remind you that, in reviewing the case as it is my duty to do, in weighing up the arguments and counter-arguments produced in the course of this trial, I cannot relieve you of any part of your responsibility to decide as to their weight. It is up to you, and to you alone, to draw your own conclusions.

"This being clear, let us come straight to the point.

"What is this case all about?

"As a result of an artificial insemination experimentally performed on the female of a manlike species, recently discovered, the defendant found himself the father of a small hybrid creature, which he killed deliberately on the day of its birth.

"You have to judge whether, in doing so, the defendant has or has not committed a murder.

"Now murder, as a matter of law, is 'the intentional killing of a human being,' so for murder to have been committed, the defendant's act must be proved to have conformed in all points to that definition.

"You cannot, therefore, in this case, return a verdict of guilty unless you have first satisfied yourselves that

187

the following three points have been proved beyond all reasonable doubt:

"First, that the prisoner did kill the deceased.

"Second, that he did so intentionally.

"Third, that the creature thus intentionally killed was a human being.

"With regard to the first two points, you need not, it seems, feel any hesitation. The prisoner claims the responsibility for his act, he admits and proclaims that it was intentional. All the evidence you heard confirmed that this is so.

"The third point, however, seems much less clear.

"Professor Knaatsch asserted that the deceased was a human being. He adduced as proof of this that the species to which it belongs can chip stone, make fire, talk a little; and has adopted the upright posture. The Professors Cocks and Hanson support his view, though for different reasons.

"In opposition to that view, Professor Eatons asserts that we cannot be dealing with a human being, since the foot of the deceased is of a conformation that has never appeared in any creature that stands in the evolutionary line of descent terminating in man.

"This was also the opinion expressed by Dr. Figgins.

"The prosecution has assured you that it is not your task to arbitrate in a dispute of experts; even less, however, to wash your hands of the whole case by an acquittal that would leave out of account the terrible consequences that might ensue. Your task, says the Crown, is to find the accused guilty of murder with premeditation since, legally and judicially, no doubt exists on that point.

"I do not think, however, that you can unhesitatingly

188

follow such advice. On the contrary, I think that you must satisfy yourselves, before deciding on the guilt of the accused, that the third condition which must obtain if there is to be legal murder, has really been fulfilled. In other words, you must be satisfied beyond all reasonable doubt that the deceased was a human being.

"Beyond all reasonable doubt. This expression has come up over and again in the course of this trial. It is my task to enlighten you on the exact meaning of those two words.

"What, in effect, constitutes a 'reasonable doubt'?

"A dangerous confusion may arise on this point.

"The doubt may reside in the facts. For example, when an accused person is noticed on the scene of the crime but there is no conclusive evidence to prove that he committed it. In that case there does exist a reasonable doubt.

"Or the doubt may reside in the mind. For instance, if a juror's memory is at fault because of the vast number of facts presented in evidence, thus making it difficult for the juror to reach a clear understanding of the case. One cannot then speak of a reasonable doubt. In that case the jury must ask, as often as necessary, for further explanations, and if these, in the last resort, are still insufficient to enlighten them, it is open to the jury to declare itself unqualified to judge.

"If therefore you consider that there is a reasonable doubt in the facts, you must disregard completely the possible consequences of an acquittal, in however frightful or alarming a light the prosecution may have presented them. You must find the prisoner not guilty.

"If, on the contrary, you consider that the doubt lies, not in the facts, but in your understanding of them, then

189

I cannot but repeat the Crown's exhortation to you: if the defendant stood here alone, if it were a question of your decision affecting only him, Christian compassion might be admissible in the event of doubt. But in the case before you, the consequences would be too grave to permit of an acquittal on the simple grounds of convenience, and it is certainly your duty as human beings to take into account those dreadful consequences.

"Nevertheless, to return a verdict against the prisoner while doubt remained in your mind would be equally unacceptable. In fact, you would thereby create a no less perilous precedent for the future administration of our justice. For if you were to send a possibly innocent man to his death, convicted not in punishment of his crime, but in consideration of the potential social or political consequences which his acquittal might entail you would be undermining the very foundations of British justice."

After a brief pause, the judge continued:

"To sum up, then, I agree with the prosecution that the doubt cannot reside in the facts themselves. They are what they are, and the tropi is what he is. His nature is a given fact that is not dependent on us. Like the Crown, therefore, I consider that if doubt there is, it resides only in the understandable confusion caused by learned disputes. Consequently, I hold that the prosecution is right in saying that a doubt of this kind does not warrant mental laziness resulting in leniency regardless of the consequences.

"On the other hand, I concur with the defense that you cannot, in all conscience, convict the prisoner without

190

first being certain that the three premises of a murder have been fulfilled.

"It therefore seems indispensable that, before pronouncing yourselves one way or another, you should first have settled in your own minds the initial question of the nature of the deceased: ape or human being.

"Only when you are certain of that, can you decide one way or another.

"Failing such certainty, it must be feared that whatever verdict you return will prove a tragic and fatal blunder."

He paused again and then added:

"You are now, ladies and gentlemen of the jury, in possession of all the facts of the case. It remains for you to consider your verdict and to answer, in one word or in two, the question that will presently be put to you: do you find the prisoner at the bar guilty or not guilty?

"Members of the jury, you may now retire."

Mr. Justice Draper thereupon rose, left the courtroom, and unburdened himself of the wig beneath which he was perspiring. As for the public, it unburdened itself of the constraint of silence in a hubbub of conversation that burst with the sound of the sea breaking on rocks.

∽

As soon as the hearing was resumed, the jury returned to the court. The foreman asked, on behalf of them all, for some explanations. He was hardly less pale than the slip of paper that was trembling in his hand.

"We are already agreed," he said, "on the main thing, on the . . . er . . . crime. No doubt on that score. There

191

only remains one thing to decide, as you said: whether or not the tropis are human. But that's just what we know nothing about."

"Quite so," said Sir Arthur. "Well?"

"Well, could you, my lord, tell us . . . what exactly you think about it?"

"That is impossible. I am here to throw light on the facts, on the points of law. I cannot have an opinion. And even if I had one, it would be most improper for me to express it."

The elderly juryman, tall and spare, with white hair curling round his small, shiny, pink pate, moved his lantern jaw sideways once or twice before saying:

"In that case, we thought if we might at least have . . . if you would just recall to our minds how . . . how man is generally defined, I mean in everyday usage . . . the proper, legal definition . . . surely that . . . er . . . that doesn't exceed your powers?"

"Indeed it doesn't," said the judge, smilingly. "However, such a legal definition would first of all have to exist. It is odd, perhaps, but the fact is that it doesn't.

The old man stared at him stupidly for a moment, then he asked:

"There isn't one?"

"No."

"But, I mean, that isn't possible."

"It's odd, I grant you, I said so before. Though actually quite in keeping with our national character. Anyway, there isn't one."

"Neither in this country nor anywhere else?"

"Nowhere at all. Not even in France, where every-

192

thing is defined and codified, down to who owns the egg that the hen will lay in the neighbor's garden."

"But that's incredible," said the old juryman after a moment. "Are we to believe that everything is, as you say, defined and codified, even the tiniest thing, except . . . why, just ourselves?"

"That's perfectly correct," said the judge.

"But look here, my lord . . . . All the time that man's been existing, nobody's ever? . . . Everything's been thought of . . . laid down and defined, except just that? Isn't that rather as if one hadn't thought of anything at all? As if one'd put a whole lot of carts before the horse?"

The judge smiled. His hands described a movement of restrained helplessness.

"Because after all," continued the juryman, "if you don't know . . . exactly . . . I mean to say, if people haven't even agreed . . . on, why, on us, on what we . . . well, how the dickens can they agree on anything?"

"That is perhaps," admitted the judge, still smiling, "why we all agree so badly. However, we are straying, and time is getting on."

"Pardon me, my lord," said the old man, "but really . . . even for . . . what we have on hand now, isn't that rather . . . a confoundedly big gap?"

"You might fill it," suggested the judge.

"*We* might?"

"In fact, if you don't, I very much fear that you won't be able to form a sound opinion of this case. In order to define the tropis, you will certainly have to define man first."

"But if nobody's ever done it, how do you expect

us to, my lord? We'd at least need someone to help us!"

"That's precisely what I'm here for, to answer your questions."

"But when I ask you, you answer that you don't know!"

"I am here to refresh your memory on everything that was said in court on this subject, and to explain to you anything that you did not understand."

"But," protested the old juryman in annoyance, "we remember perfectly what was said, and I think we understood it quite well too. The trouble is that . . . well, if all those professors had at least agreed among themselves . . . . But they never stopped bickering . . . . So how do you expect us to manage . . . ."

"Nevertheless you'll have to," said the judge. "And, as a matter of fact, without more delay. If you do not return your verdict within half an hour, you will have to resume your deliberations tomorrow."

The jury filed out of court again, preceded by their foreman who was shaking his curly white head. He was still shaking it when they came back twenty minutes later.

"We are getting nowhere," he announced. "In fact, it's getting worse and worse. The more we talk, the less we agree. A few are for, some against, and all the others say they don't know. As for me, I'm completely lost."

"You must urge your fellow jurors to come to a decision," said the judge. "There are still ten minutes left."

At the end of the ten minutes the foreman returned, followed by the rest of the jury, and declared:

"We are definitely agreed that we cannot agree."

And he said no more.

194

The judge waited a while before speaking.

"Perhaps you were short of time, after all," he said at last. "I therefore suggest that you continue your deliberations tomorrow —"

"It's quite useless," said the foreman. "We are fully agreed."

"Not to agree?"

"Not to agree. We declare ourselves unqualified to judge."

Sir Arthur again let some time pass before announcing:

"Under these circumstances I regret that I am bound to discharge the jury. A new trial will therefore be ordered before another jury in the next Sessions. The hearing is over."

The public had to see the judge actually leave the court before they grasped what had happened. At first a dazed silence hung over the courtroom. And then it burst in a wild and varied flutter of emotions. The venerable oak panels resounded to a hullabaloo tempered only by respect for those august walls. People jumped up, called to each other in suppressed shouts that were full of excitement or dismay. Frances too had risen. She was straining, above the sea of heads, to catch her husband's eye. He had only a moment ago been led back into court for the verdict, and was already being shepherded out. Their glances met. And Douglas, raising his two clasped hands to the ceiling, gave the boxer's gleeful greeting on being declared the winner in the ring.

Chapter 15

THE LORD PRIVY SEAL'S WORRIES AND THOSE OF
THE BRITISH WOOL MANUFACTURERS. "TROPI OR
NOT TROPI." MR. JUSTICE DRAPER SUGGESTS THAT
THE MATTER BE REFERRED TO PARLIAMENT. HOW
A VENERABLE TRADITION IS BY-PASSED. THE COM-
MITTEE OF INQUIRY IS SET UP. DISAGREEMENT
WITHIN THE COMMITTEE. GROWING DISCORD.
THE BENEFICIAL EFFECT OF IRRECONCILABLE
OPINIONS. FRANCES MAKES A PAINFUL CON-
FESSION. SOLIDARITY WITH THE HUMAN SPECIES.
ESSENTIAL DIFFERENCE BETWEEN MAN AND
BEAST. THE CONVENIENCE OF SILENCE.

SIR Arthur Draper fully expected a summons of some
sort from high quarters. Would it come from the Home
Secretary? or the Attorney General? In fact, it was the
Lord Privy Seal — minister of no affairs in particular —
who asked the old judge to come and see him at his club.

On his way through Green Park, Sir Arthur thought:
"This means we shall probably talk of everything except justice. In a way, that suits me well . . . ." He went
on to think: "So I probably shan't have to explain the

196

somewhat . . . er . . . unorthodox way in which I steered the trial towards deadlock and the jury into bewilderment . . . . It looks rather as if *they* want to ask something of me. Something a trifle unorthodox too, no doubt . . . . So I'll have some trumps in my hand. But shall I know how to play them, eh? I'm hardly accustomed to diplomacy . . . ."

The Lord Privy Seal did not keep him waiting. He greeted him with an easygoing "Hallo!" slapped him familiarly on the shoulder, and led him towards a secluded corner where they both sat down. After a few affable words. the minister handed the judge a batch of newspapers.

"Have you had a look at the foreign papers?"

Sir Arthur shook his head and read, not without amusement, the tall headlines of the Chicago *Daily Post: TROPI OR NOT TROPI?* The article gave a sarcastic summary of the trial and severely criticized the British for their formalism and lack of resilience, which enabled any slightly unusual case that came along to effectively hamstring British justice. In France, *Le Parisien*, under the headline: *TROPI SOIT QUI MAL Y PENSE*, expressed similar views, but in a lighter, less mocking vein, and went on to ask its readers with clear-sighted humor: "If you had been a juryman, what would YOU have done?" *Rude Pravo*, of Prague, wrote ironically: *TWELVE SKULLS IN A CLEFT STICK*, and recalled all kinds of silly brain teasers: if you could rescue only one person in a shipwreck, would it be your mother, your wife, your daughter? Such are the moral dilemmas in which bourgeois justice entangles its jurymen. . . .

197

No one seemed to have noticed the old judge's little maneuvers.

Sir Arthur put down the papers and waited.

"Was it really impossible," asked the minister, "to get a sensible verdict brought in?"

The judge pointed out that the laws of the land hardly empowered a judge to coerce a jury . . . .

"But did you really . . . do your utmost?" asked the minister. "Did you really bring all your influence to bear?"

"In favor of what?" asked Sir Arthur gently.

"In favor of getting a verdict returned."

"A verdict in whose favor?" Sir Arthur asked again.

The minister stirred a little in his armchair.

"It is surely not for me to . . ."

"Nor for me," said Sir Arthur. "If the judge stops being impartial, why have a jury? Moreover, it would be an insult to the intelligence of our fellow countrymen. Let French justice keep its citizens in leading strings if they like. You don't approve, I presume, the law in force over there since the German occupation, whereby the jury's deliberations are presided over by the judge?"

"Certainly not, certainly not!" the Lord Privy Seal hastened to assure him. "However, it's a confounded nuisance, this business . . . ." He was playing with an ash tray, which seemed to absorb his interest. "Have you at least read our own papers?"

"I've glanced at them. Anyway, a judge cannot take public opinion into account."

"Opinion is pretty excited . . . a bit feverish. One oughtn't to . . . What do you think will happen next time, with a fresh jury?"

"What do you expect to happen?" asked Sir Arthur. "Very possibly, the same thing."

"That's out of the question!" cried the minister.

Sir Arthur mildly raised his hands and let them fall again.

There was a lengthy silence. Then the minister broached what was apparently a new subject.

"My colleague of the Board of Trade called on me yesterday," he said.

Sir Arthur assumed an air of polite attention.

"He told me . . . naturally this is strictly between ourselves . . . . He pointed out . . . I merely tell you this as a matter of interest . . . . It goes without saying that your high office . . . that you cannot enter into considerations . . . . well, anyway, it may be useful for you to know, just for your information, I repeat . . . that certain circles are pretty worried."

The minister fidgeted with the ash tray, looking deeply absorbed.

"It is impossible to overlook the fact . . . when the prosperity of a huge branch of our industry is gravely threatened . . . you are not unaware, I suppose" — and at last he raised his eyes to Sir Arthur's — "of certain Australian designs on the tropis?"

Sir Arthur nodded. The minister continued:

"It is a happy coincidence that . . . that the interests of our great textile industry harmonize with . . . the views expressed by the Crown. Profoundly humanitarian views, are they not? Profoundly. And even if . . . if your impartiality prevents your publicly subscribing to them . . . it is highly desirable, is it not, from every point of view, that the tropis should be definitely held to be human?"

There was a long pause before Sir Arthur replied:

"It might be," he said at length.

He paused again, then resumed:

"It might be — but on one condition."

He broke off again, and the minister, with a gesture that ill hid his impatience, invited him to go on.

"On condition that their being human could never again be called in doubt."

"Explain yourself," said the minister.

"Even if a jury," said Sir Arthur, "declared the accused guilty — which is hardly likely to happen at present — what would that prove? That he is held, *in law*, to have committed a crime against his son. But the *nature* of that son would still be open to doubt. In any case, the doubt would still exist as regards the tropis in general. That would be to nobody's advantage, it seems to me."

The minister showed by a glance that he was waiting for the sequel.

"The accused would be sent to the gallows or to prison," said the judge, "but once this is done, what could prevent the Takura Company from employing the tropis as beasts of burden in their spinning mills? Unless a new action was brought, even less clear than the previous one. And brought by whom, anyway?"

"So what do you suggest?"

Sir Arthur pretended to ponder deeply before replying.

"For a verdict to serve a useful purpose, it would, you see, it would be imperative that it should be based on unassailable legal foundations."

"I see," said the minister. "But what foundations?"

"The one the jury vainly clamored for."

"That is to say . . . ?"

200

"A clear and precise legal definition of the human being."

The minister opened his eyes wide. He hesitated before asking:

"Why . . . there isn't one?"

"That's precisely," said Sir Arthur with a discreet smile, "what the foreman of the jury asked me in amazement."

"Fantastic!" said the minister. "How is it possible?"

"This sort of definition isn't the strong point of us Englishmen. In fact, we're dead against them."

"I know . . . what I meant is, how is it possible that the French for instance . . . or the Germans, my dear fellow, take the Germans! Is it conceivable that German scholars can write their laborious tomes about things they haven't first defined?"

Sir Arthur smiled.

"Anyway," said the minister, "it's a damned nuisance for us now. What can be done? How do you think we could get hold of . . ."

"I think," said Sir Arthur, "that it is a matter for Parliament."

The minister's eyes lighted up. At last this annoying business was getting onto familiar, well-trodden ground. But he grimaced:

"Just think of our good old M.P.s! They'll be horrified, as you said yourself. A definition! Clear-cut and precise! A definition of man! We'll never get them to . . ."

"That's not so certain. You saw the jury's reaction at the trial. Remember your own a moment ago. That's the marvelous side of this affair. Even we English are overcoming our instinctive distaste and feel impelled to . . ."

201

"You like your little joke, Sir Arthur," said the minister with a sour smile.

"I'd never take the liberty . . . ."

"You were in earnest?"

"Dead earnest. The need to define the person, the human person, once and for all, has become so urgent that even Parliament will accept the task, I think."

The minister thought this over for a while. Then he said:

"Perhaps you are right. . . . It may not be impossible, after all, to . . . have a question put . . . preferably by someone of our own party . . . yes, blaming us for . . . having let this case turn into a farce . . . ."

He was biting his lips with a thoughtful smile. He seemed almost to have forgotten Sir Arthur. He remembered him only when he heard him suggesting:

"The debate in the Commons must not seem to have any too close connection with the trial. You realize, of course, that as long as the case is *sub judice*, any discussion likely to affect the verdict one way or another would be quite inadmissible."

"Oh damn! . . . Why, that . . . that rather upsets the applecart?"

"Not necessarily, if proper precautions are taken."

"Would you advise us?"

"I could not claim to more legal knowledge than the Attorney General or . . ."

"To be sure, to be sure. But they are short of time. Come on, it's agreed. You'll guide our steps."

He got up. The judge rose too. They walked in silence over the thick carpet. After a moment the minister said:

202

"Tell me . . . counsel for the defense . . . isn't he an M.P.?"

"Jameson? Yes, indeed," said the judge.

"Won't we run into trouble there?" suggested the minister. "I mean . . . mightn't he . . . I don't know . . . throw a spanner in the works?"

"I don't think so," said the judge with a smile. "On the contrary, if we go about it in the right way, I believe we'll have him on our side."

The minister stopped. He opened his eyes and wrinkled his brow at the same time.

"But . . ." he started to say with some discomfiture, "let's be quite clear about it. . . . If, as we hope, the tropis are ultimately declared human beings, won't his client stand a good chance of being hanged?"

"Don't say I told you," said Sir Arthur, "but, between ourselves, whatever the outcome, the accused no longer runs much risk, I think."

His smile broadened as he added:

"Unless, of course, his lawyer is a greater fool than I bargained for."

འ

Things did not go without a hitch.

The outset was encouraging: a question was raised in the House by a young M.P. who, with a beautiful Oxford accent, attacked the judicature with shafts of wit, epigrams and quotations abundantly drawn from Shakespeare and the Bible.

In the absence of the Home Secretary, the Lord Privy Seal answered with humor and dignity. He bravely defended Her Majesty's judiciary, declaring that none could have discharged their task better or as well, and exposed the foolishness of the press which had failed to remark on the one salient fact: the absence of any precise definition of the human being in all the legal codes of the world.

The young member asked what the government proposed to do to prevent the same cause from indefinitely producing the same effect.

In his reply, the minister indicated that far from being taken by surprise, the government had given the matter their mature consideration. They had come to the conclusion, he said, that it was within the powers of Parliament to repair this astonishing omission. The government proposed that a commission should be set up in order to obtain, with the aid of representatives of science and the law, a legal definition of man. The occasion moved him to a brilliant flight of eloquence. He said that Great Britain, having taught the world democracy, would now lay the foundation stone of another sublime edifice. "Imagine," he said, "the consequences of our action, if such a definition should one day pass beyond the framework of British legislation and be incorporated in international law. For if what constitutes the essence of man comes to be legally defined, will not our obligations towards man be defined by the same stroke: since anything that threatened that essence would automatically be a menace to humanity. All the rights and duties of man, of social groups, of societies and nations, towards one another, in all latitudes, of all creeds, would for the first time be founded on the very nature of Man, on the irrefutable elements that distinguish him from the Beast. No longer would those rights and duties rely on utilitarian and hence destructible conventions, on philosophical and hence assailable theories, or on arbitrary, hence corruptible and changing traditions — let alone on the blind fury of passions.

"For do we not often see that what is a crime for one group of people is none for their neighbors or their foes? — who may even extol it as a duty or an honor, as we could see in the case of the Nazis? And was it not useless to create in Nuremberg a new law which was not, in its very foundation, acknowledged equally by all? For today we find that, in the name of German traditions, the friends of the condemned drag that law from its lofty eminence as a safeguard of Human Rights down to the disgraceful level of a safeguard of Human Might — and we cannot crush them with the proof of their abject mistake. That is why today we see the Nuremberg laws, in spite of all the hopes that went to their making, gradually dissolving into shadows, and in those shadows new crimes prepared.

"Now, an opportunity is offered us, to us, Her Majesty's loyal Commons — if we can but rise to the task — of bringing to divided mankind a basic, legal definition of what distinguishes man from the beast. A definition that will not prove or disprove any existing conceptions — be they political, philosophic or religious, but which will be the single root from which spring all those varied and divergent branches, even when they seem to contradict or claim to exclude each other. In other words, we shall supply the keynote which will turn all those jarring discords into one grand harmony."

He raised his voice:

205

"That opportunity lies now within our grasp. It may frighten us, it may even shock us with its challenge to our customs, to our traditional caution. But the greatness of the task condemns faintheartedness, and, as Shakespeare said:

> What custom wills, in all things should we do't,
> The dust on antique time would lie unswept,
> And mountainous error be too highly heap'd
> For truth to o'er-peer . . . ."

There was some cheering, as the Lord Privy Seal sat down, and the Home Secretary, who had come in during his speech, was seen warmly shaking his hand.

Before the government proposal was put to the vote, Mr. B. K. Jameson rose and said:

"The government's initiative in this matter is to their credit, and as a member of the House I feel bound to congratulate them. But it so happens that I am also a member of the bar, and one, moreover who, holding a brief for Douglas Templemore, is particularly interested in the question of the definition of man. I thus find myself torn by a moral conflict which must be felt, I am sure, to some extent, by the House as a whole. For if we legislate on a definition of man while the case of Douglas Templemore is still *sub judice*, it is incontestable that this definition will substantially affect the verdict of the jury and hence the fate of the accused. Is not this contrary to the best interests of justice, and would it not be advisable to postpone action until the end of this case?"

The Home Secretary replied that he did not share the honorable member's fears.

206

"It is not a question," he said, "of our deciding anything about the nature of the tropis. Our limited and exclusive task is to define the human being. If that definition, subsequently, should turn out to have some effect on certain legal proceedings, it could only be an indirect effect; just as the delineation of a frontier, in the course of negotiations for a peace treaty, may ultimately have an indirect effect on a legal dispute about neighbors' adjoining walls. There could obviously be no question of postponing a peace treaty between two nations until such time as that particular case was settled.

"Similarly, the definition of man is a matter of national and world-wide interest. Its urgency has no doubt been brought into prominence by the peculiarity of a case in progress, but it far transcends it in every way."

Mr. Jameson was asked by the Speaker if he still maintained his objection. He replied that he was pleased to admit, both as a jurist and as a parliamentarian, the undeniable cogency of the Home Secretary's argument, and therefore withdrew his objection.

This opened the way for a lively debate as to how Parliament was to set about discharging this unusual and impressive task. Should a Royal Commission be appointed? A Committee of Inquiry be set up? Or was it more prudent for Parliament to leave the task, on the contrary, to an unofficial body, such as the Royal Society?

An old member declared that man being composed of mind and body, he surely could not be better defined than by the Lords Spiritual and Temporal. Another said that since a legal definition was wanted, it would be absurd not to appeal quite simply to the legal lights of

207

the bench and the bar under the chairmanship of the Lord Chief Justice. Another said it was the business of the Queen and of her Privy Council, which surely came into its own in just such an emergency. Yet another suggested a congress of anthropologists, another again a congress of psychologists. Someone asked whether the B.B.C. could not be requested to conduct a referendum.

The suggestion that was ultimately adopted revealed the British genius for compromise at its highest in that, while contenting no one, it was acceptable to all. The choice fell upon the Royal College of Moral and Spiritual Sciences, an august body which counted among its members personalities of all callings and walks of life. This body was charged to form a committee, to which were to be nominated, informally by the various parties, certain members of the House, thus giving it a semiofficial character.

As a result, Sir Kenneth Summer, a noted back-bencher and active member of the college, could soon after announce in the Commons the formation of a "Committee for the Study of a Specification of the Human Species with a View to the Legal Definition of Man." For the sake of convenience, this was later generally referred to as the Summer Committee, after its chairman. Sir Arthur Draper was invited to assist the Committee, both as a distinguished jurist and as a sort of surety, by his presence, of the legality of their undertaking. It was decided to meet on Tuesdays and Fridays in the famous library of the Royal College of Moral and Spiritual Sciences, which had once been Cecil Rhode's small reading room.

208

And then it was that the difficulties began.

ભ

It became clear, in effect, that every member of the Committee had come to it with a preconceived view on the subject, to which he clung tenaciously. Lord Humpleton, the *doyen* of the Committee, who was asked to open the proceedings, declared that in his opinion the best possible definition had been given by Wesley who, he reminded his fellow members, had shown that reason, though generally supposed to be a distinguishing feature of man, could not be so regarded. Indeed, many animals give proof of intelligence, whereas ideas as aberrant as fetishism and sorcery, alien to animals, scarcely plead in favor of human wisdom. The true difference, said Wesley, is that we are formed to know God and they are not.

A little Quaker lady, slim and graying, with candid eyes behind thick glasses, asked to be heard, and in a soft, almost quavering voice said that she did not see how we could presume to know what was going on in a dog's or a chimpanzee's heart, and how one could be sure that they did not know God in their fashion.

"But look here," protested Lord Humpleton, "they can't possibly! I mean, it stands to reason!"

The little Quaker lady said that assertion was no proof, and another, timid-looking, member suggested in a mild voice that it would be rash, moreover, to deny the fetish worshippers all benefit of reason: they merely exercised it badly, he assured the gathering, just as a banker who goes bankrupt may practice finance badly, but is yet more of a financier then, say, a midshipman of

209

H.M.S. Victory. "It seems to me," he concluded, "that we should, on the contrary, make it our starting point that man is endowed with reason."

"And where exactly do you make reason start?" he was asked ironically by a very smartly dressed gentleman with impeccably starched collar and cuffs.

"That is precisely what we must define," said the shy gentleman.

But Lord Humpleton said that if the idea of God were to be left out of the definition of man, his own religious convictions would not allow him to take any further part in the work of the Committee.

Sir Kenneth Summer, in the chair, reminded him that the government had explicitly stated that the definition to be formulated by the Committee must be acceptable to all schools of thought and opinion. Lord Humpleton need therefore have no fear that the idea of God would be missing from it. However, an exclusively theological definition could no more meet the case since it would fail to satisfy the large number of agnostics to be found not only on the Continent, but also in the British Isles.

A portly gentleman with a heavy white mustache — a former colonel in the Indian Army who had had resounding *affaires* with ladies of note — said that what he was going to say might appear extravagant; but that, in the course of his long and intimate acquaintance with men and animals, he had come to the conclusion that one thing and one thing alone was entirely typical of man, and that was sexual perversion. He added that he thought that man was the only animal in creation that had, for instance, founded brilliant societies on homosexuality.

A gentleman-farmer from Hampshire asked Colonel

Strang whether, according to him, the basic peculiarity lay in the existence of those brilliant societies — in which case what needed defining was man's urge to found civilizations — or whether it lay in homosexuality: for in the latter case he was sorry to have to inform the colonel that homosexual couples, both male and female, were quite common among ducks.

His own opinion, he added, was that you could get nowhere if you remained within "closed" fields of studies, like zoology, psychology, theology, and all the rest. Man is an "open" complex, he said, existing only in his relationship to other men and to things. He is determined by his environment, which he in turn determines, and it is this constant interplay which in the long run produces history. And outside history all is but a figment of the brain.

The gentleman with the cuffs ran a ringed finger round the inside of his collar as he said that his honorable colleague seemed to have contracted, on his Hampshire estate, an acute form of Marxian indigestion, and that if he'd set out to turn not only the Committee but the entire British government into Marxists, he would need a little more time than the Committee had at its disposal. The little Quaker woman said in her gentle, quavering voice that you need not be a Marxist to think as her colleague did, but that if what he said seemed substantially true, it did not, practically speaking, lead them anywhere. For it would still be necessary to explain why that interplay does not occur in animal societies. If man has a changing history and the animals have not, it is because there is something peculiar to man, and it was this that had to be defined.

Sir Kenneth asked her if she had any view to propound. She said that she most certainly had. "Man," she said, "is the only animal capable of entirely selfless acts. In other words, goodness and charity are peculiar to man and to him alone."

Lord Humpleton asked rather sarcastically how she knew that animals were incapable of unselfish impulses since she herself had claimed a moment ago that they might possibly know God? The gentleman-farmer capped it by remarking that his own dog had died in a fire because he had thrown himself into the flames to save a child. And anyway, even if it were shown that these feelings are peculiar to man, it would remain, as she herself had said, to discover what was the source of this difference.

The gentleman with the cuffs took the floor to say that as far as he was concerned it mattered very little whether there was a legal definition of man or not. For five hundred thousand years, he said man had got on without being defined; or rather he had invented for himself changing conceptions which, in their day, had served the civilizations he had built. Why not let him continue in this way? One thing alone mattered, he claimed: the traces left by those civilizations as they disappeared. In a word — art. "This," he said, "is the characteristic feature of man, from Cro-Magnon days down to our own."

"But," asked the Quaker lady, "does it leave you altogether unmoved that thousands of tropis, supposing they're human, may be reduced to slavery; and, supposing they are apes, that an innocent man may be hanged?"

212

The gentleman answered that, as a matter of fact, from a somewhat loftier standpoint, it left him perfectly unmoved. Life crawls with injustices. The most you can flatter yourself on doing is reducing them to a minimum. To that end we have laws, traditions, customs, forms. The main thing is to apply them. That they may be more or less well applied is inherent in the indeterminate nature of what is just and unjust, and this we have not the power to change.

The gentleman-farmer said that this was of course open to debate, though he himself was not far from sharing this view. But he asked his colleague to give him a definition of art. For, he said, if he wanted to use art to define man, art itself must be defined first.

The gentleman with the cuffs replied that art being a unique and self-evident manifestation, immediately recognizable by all, there was no need to define it.

The gentleman-farmer said that, in that case, man being a self-evident and immediately recognizable species, there was no need to define him either.

The gentleman with the cuffs said that that was precisely what he himself had declared earlier.

Sir Kenneth pointed out that the Committee was meeting not in order to establish that man needed no definition but rather to attempt a definition.

He said that the first session had perhaps not advanced matters very much, but that it had at least afforded an opportunity for a frank exchange of interesting opinions.

Then he closed the meeting.

෮

When the next meeting broke up, members seemed

213

somewhat less composed. Beneath his silky mustache, the gentleman with the cuffs was smiling in a forced, rather jaundiced way at one corner of his mouth. Old Lord Humpleton's pale cheeks were twitching convulsively. And hadn't the little Quaker lady actually traces of tears behind her thick glasses? The gentleman-farmer's forehead showed beads of perspiration, while Colonel Strang was chewing nervously his thick white mustache. Good-bys were said with hollow politeness, and the chairman, Sir Kenneth Summer, found himself alone with Sir Arthur Draper, to whom he confided with a touch of alarm:

"It seems to me we are a little less advanced than last time."

Sir Arthur confessed that he had the same impression.

Sir Kenneth said that he was beginning to wonder whether the members of the Committee had not such irreconcilable views that it might perhaps be difficult . . .

Sir Arthur said that he did not think them as irreconcilable as might appear at first glance.

In a voice betraying considerable relief Sir Kenneth said that he was happy to hear Sir Arthur say so even though his views might be overoptimistic. As for himself, he added, he really couldn't quite see how . . .

"Actually," said Sir Arthur, "that's a very good sign."

"What is? That I don't quite see . . . ?"

"No, no: that those opinions seem irreconcilable."

"A good sign?"

"Certainly. If everybody thought more or less the same, the Committee would have whisked out a definition in two shakes of a duck's tail. Do you think it would have proved a sound one?"

"Why not? Time has nothing to do with it."

"Perhaps. But there's every likelihood that a definition of man produced by a dozen Englishmen in prompt unanimity would have turned out to be nothing more than a definition of *Homo Britannicus*. That isn't what is wanted of you."

"By Jove! There's something in what you say."

"Whereas the very gulf that separates your colleagues' ideas at the moment will gradually force them, in the course of stormy debates perhaps, to strip their conceptions of all that divides them, until they have finally reached their lowest common denominator, the hidden core of all their ideas."

"That's perfectly true."

"You will need patience, that's all."

"Quite . . . quite. And that's not my strong point, I'm afraid."

It certainly wasn't Sir Kenneth's strong point.

From one meeting to another his authority slipped. More and more often he appealed to Sir Arthur to arbitrate. Within a short time, Sir Arthur, by general consent, was practically guiding the debates, singlehanded.

During the same period, Lady Draper had got to know Frances. The old lady had said to her niece:

"You keep her well hidden, that protégée of yours."

She knew the term would annoy her. Frances needed no protector! She was quite capable of looking after herself! her niece had indeed retorted indignantly. "Then why do you hide her?" asked her aunt.

"I'm not hiding her," her niece replied, "but I thought . . . would it be quite the right thing?"

215

"Would what?"

"Well, to bring her here. . . . Uncle Arthur was her husband's judge. He may be so again. . . . I wonder whether it would be quite proper. . . ."

"What have I got to do with all that?"

"Come, come, Aunt Gertrude!"

"Am I going to judge her fool of a husband?"

"No, but still . . ."

"You bring her here to tea tomorrow."

Before accepting, Frances visited Douglas in prison and asked his advice. What could the old lady want of her?

"You must go," said Douglas. "Draper won't be my judge again. If there were any doubt about that, he wouldn't have agreed to be on the Summer Committee. You must go!" he repeated, with sudden excitement. "I'd give a lot to know what old Draper thinks, what's going on in that Committee, and what will come of it all!"

Frances, with lips closed, looked at her husband across the table of the prison parlor. Then she murmured:

"It's awful, my love, but I daren't tell you what I'm thinking."

"Frances! But why, good Lord?"

"Because . . . because . . . I am torn to pieces inside myself. I loathe what I'm thinking. Yes, I loathe it. It makes me ill. And yet I can't help thinking it."

"Frances, I've never seen you like that. What's happened? You are hiding something from me?"

She shook her lovely, soft fair hair with childish fervor.

"You must have looked like that when you were lying to your father," said Douglas, teasing her gently.

216

She laughed, but at the same time a little tear ran down her nose.

"I'm ashamed of myself," she confessed.

Douglas did not press her. He looked at her and his smile was so full of trust and tenderness that she could not keep back a second tear. She caught a third one by sniffing like a little girl. And she laughed again:

"I amuse you, but if you knew . . ."

"Well," said Douglas, "I shall know."

She faltered all the same.

"You think I'm stronger than I am," she said at last.

"But you *are* strong!"

"Yes, but not so strong as you think."

"We'll see about that," said Douglas.

She looked at him across the table. She stared at him, at his kindly, rather pale face beneath his rumpled saffron shock of hair.

"I can't," she said with a sudden, heartbreaking sigh. "It's so very much the wrong moment. . . ."

"But you will be more unhappy if you keep it to yourself."

"Yes."

"I'll tell you what's the matter," said Douglas.

She mutely opened her eyes and mouth like a goldfish.

"You no longer think I am right," he said with deep seriousness.

"I do!" she shouted.

She had clutched the sides of the table, as if she wanted to shake it.

"Don't ever believe that! Never, Douglas! Promise me. . . . Never!" she cried.

"With all my heart," said Douglas, relieved. "Never."

217

"You know I'll always love and admire you just as much, whatever happens, and even more if they want to . . . if they ever . . . ever decided . . . I'll make you a silken ladder," she said smiling, "and smuggle it to you in a pie. I'll flee with you. I'll hide you in a cave. . . . I'll become a murderer myself, perhaps, to defend you . . . . You know that, don't you?"

"I know. But . . ."

She said nothing. He repeated with gentle insistence: "But?"

"But it's true that it won't be the same any more," she whispered, just loud enough for him to hear.

"What won't be the same?"

"I'd love you as much, but no longer in the same . . . the same . . . crystalline fashion."

"You, too, would consider me a . . . murderer?"

She mutely nodded "yes."

Douglas remained silent for a while, in order to grasp it completely.

"That's funny," he said at length.

He gazed at her with a twinkle of amusement, as if what she had said were only a little quaint.

"*I* won't," he added.

Frances's face lighted up with a gleam of hope and expectancy.

"You won't? Not you? Even if the tropis are human?"

"Even then," said Douglas. "I can't quite explain it to you, like that, on the spot. But I am sure, whatever happens, that I've only killed a little animal. Perhaps because, roughly speaking . . . it's as if . . . as if, during the war, I'd killed a German from East Prussia and

218

someone said to me, 'Yes, but today he'd be a Pole. So you've killed one of our allies.' I'd jolly well know it wasn't true."

Frances thought this over for a moment, and she sighed:

"That isn't the same thing."

She shook her head gently, her eyes on the ground.

"Your German was first one thing, and then another. Whereas your little troplet . . . he was nothing. He's still nothing. What they'll decide he was, that's what he'll really be."

And suddenly it seemed to burst out of her:

"That's what I can't bear. Not to be able to help myself . . . if they declare . . . if it appears the tropis are human . . . not to be able to prevent it doing something to me . . . I think it's idiotic, revolting, stupidly conventional, since you, you won't have changed. You will remain exactly the same, and yet . . . whether people decide you have killed a monkey or that you have killed a man, it will make everything different for me . . . and I, I won't be able to help thinking as they do!"

"That's rather beautiful, come to think of it," said Douglas oddly.

"Beautiful?"

"Yes. It's still too muddled for me to be able to explain clearly to you what it makes me think. But first it shows . . . it shows that at bottom murder doesn't exist. Not by itself, I mean. Since it doesn't depend on what I have done but on what men — and you, and I, too, perhaps, after all — eventually decide I've done. Men, Frances, men alone. The human species. And we feel such a

219

profound solidarity with the human species that what it thinks, we can't help thinking with it. We are not free to think differently: what they decide, that's what I am, that's what you are, that's what we all are together. And we shall decide it ourselves, for ourselves alone, without bothering about the universe. That's perhaps what strikes me as beautiful. The rest, after all, is a detail. I expect I shall suffer if I see you loving me with a less crystalline flame, as you say. But after all, I should have known that it was part of the pact."

"Douglas, my darling . . ." started Frances, but the warder was approaching. "Time's up, I'm afraid," he said. "You'll have to go now." And she had to bury all she still had to say until the next day.

०↩౦

It is difficult to say to what extent Sir Arthur Draper's ideas evolved and crystallized as a result of the sort of osmosis which thereafter occurred between Douglas and him through the medium of their wives. Was he aware of it or not? What is certain is that from week to week Frances had regular news of what was going on at the Committee meetings, as her husband had wished. She passed it on to Douglas, then talked of his reaction to Lady Draper. The old lady, left to herself, pondered on it and, over breakfast, she would say to Sir Arthur:

"Are you going to the Committee meeting today?"

"Of course."

"How much longer are you going to let those silly snails grope for each other's horns?"

"I can hardly put pressure on them, my dear."

220

"Douglas said to his wife the other day that light had come to him during the trial after Captain Thropp's statement. Or was it Professor Rampole's? I don't remember."

"Perhaps after the two taken in conjunction?"

"Perhaps. Frances told me about it, but I didn't understand a thing."

"They both said, though, like you, that man wears charms, animals don't."

"Of course. But then, what?"

"Well, I suppose Templemore has deduced certain things from that."

"And have you?"

"Yes, I have, too."

"And are they the same?"

"Very possibly."

"What deductions?"

Sir Arthur hesitated. How far could his wife follow him? Or how far had she gone ahead of him, for that matter, he thought; since it was she, after all, who'd first launched those ideas . . . . He explained:

"Their statements revealed two propositions that illuminate each other:

"There is no animal species that displays even the most rudimentary signs of a metaphysical mind.

"There is no human race that does not display at least a rudimentary sign of a metaphysical mind.

"Couldn't it be that this is a decisive distinction?"

"But," cried Lady Draper, "isn't that rather like saying: 'There's no animal species that goes to the hairdresser. There's no human race that does not go, in one

221

way or another, to the hairdresser. So what distinguishes man from the beast is that he goes to the hairdresser?"

"That wouldn't be as foolish as it sounds," said Sir Arthur. "If one were to dig a little more deeply into your hairdresser story, it would be found that man looks after his appearance, while the beast doesn't. In other words, we should find underlying ideas of ritual or of beauty, both of them highly metaphysical ideas. It all boils down to this, you see, that man asks himself questions, and the beast doesn't."

"How can we tell?" asked Lady Draper.

"Well, let us say that man seems to ask himself questions, that the beast doesn't seem to. Or again, more precisely: the presence of signs of a metaphysical spirit proves that man asks himself questions; their absence suggests that the beast doesn't."

"But why?" asked Lady Draper.

"Because the metaphysical mind . . . oh, my dear, doesn't this all bore you to tears?"

"But does that matter? We are alone," said Lady Draper with a smile.

"It's boring you, all the same."

"Oh, very well, I'll ask Frances to explain it to me. What do your snails think of it?"

"They haven't got there yet."

"Why don't you ask Rampole and Captain Thropp to come and jog them up?"

"Upon my word!" said Sir Arthur. "That's a brain wave!"

When Rampole and Thropp had finished and withdrawn, Lord Humpleton exclaimed:

"Wasn't I right? They talked like Wesley!"

"Where did you get that idea from?" asked the gentleman with the cuffs.

"What distinguishes man from the beasts is prayer."

"I heard nothing of the sort!"

"Because there are none so deaf as those —" began Lord Humpleton.

"I heard him say the very opposite. Rampole said, 'The brain of man grasps the reality behind appearances. The animal does not even grasp the appearance: it cannot go beyond sensation.' "

"But Thropp proved him wrong!" Lord Humpleton retorted. "Remember Verlaine's monkey: he could tell a triangle from a parallelogram, and a parallelogram from a square, even a heap of ten beans from a heap of eleven!"

"I could perhaps resolve your difference for you," Sir Arthur gently suggested.

Sir Kenneth begged him to do so.

"In comparing man's intelligence with the beast's," said Sir Arthur, "Professor Rampole talked to us less of quantity than of quality. He even pointed out that it is always like that in nature: a small difference in quantity can produce a sudden mutation, a total change in quality. For instance, when heating water, you can add more and more calories without the water changing its state. And then, at a given moment, one single degree is enough for it to pass from the liquid state to the gaseous one. Is not that what has occurred with our forebears' intelligence? A small addition in quantity to the brain connections, — perhaps quite a minute one — and it made

223

one of those jumps which produce a total change in quality. So that . . ."

"That's a subversive view," said the gentleman with the cuffs.

"I beg your pardon?"

"I've read things of that sort in . . . oh, I don't remember. Anyway, it's rank Bolshevik materialism. It's one of the three laws of their dialectics."

"Professor Rampole," said Sir Kenneth, "is a nephew of the Bishop of Crewe. His wife is one of Canon Clayton's daughters. The canon's mother is a friend of my mother's, and Sir Peter himself is a perfectly good Christian."

The gentleman pulled at his cuffs and gazed absorbedly at the beams of the ceiling.

"Professor Rampole," continued Sir Arthur, "has specified this change in quality. The difference between the Neanderthal man's intelligence and a great ape's can't have been much in the way of quantity. But it made a vast difference to their relationship to nature: the animal continued to submit to it; man suddenly started to question it."

"Well . . . ," Lord Humpleton and the gentleman with the cuffs exclaimed together, but Sir Arthur did not let himself be interrupted.

"Now, in order to question there must be two of you — the one who questions, and the one who is questioned. Intimately bound up with nature, the animal cannot question it. That seems to be the point we are seeking. The animal is *one* with nature, while man and nature make *two*. To pass from passive unconsciousness to questioning consciousness, there had to be that schism, that

224

divorce, there had to be that wrenching away from nature. Is not that precisely the borderline? Animal before the wrench, man after it? De-natured animals, that's what we are."

Some seconds of silence passed before Colonel Strang was heard to mutter:

"That's not so silly. Explains homosexuality."

"It explains," said Sir Arthur, "why the animal needs neither fables nor amulets. It is unaware of its own ignorance. Whereas the mind of man, torn away, cut off from nature — how could it fail to be instantly plunged in darkness and terror? Man sees himself alone, abandoned, mortal, not knowing anything — the only animal on earth 'that knows but one thing, that it knows nothing' — not even what it is. How could he help inventing myths: gods or spirits in response to that ignorance, fetishes and charms in response to that helplessness? Does not the animal's very lack of those aberrant inventions prove the absence, too, of those terrified questions?"

They all looked at him without saying a word.

"But if, then, what has made the person — the conscious person and his history — is indeed that wrench, that independence, that struggle, that de-nature; if a beast, in order to be admitted into the community of man, must have taken that hard and painful step — how, by what sign at last, can we recognize that it has done so?"

There was no answer.

225

Chapter 16

HOW A HARD CRYSTAL IS TURNED INTO A JELLY-
FISH. DOUGLAS TEMPLEMORE HAS REASONS FOR
ANXIETY. JUSTICE DRAPER'S REBELLION AND
SURRENDER. A PERTINENT OBSERVATION MADE
BY PROFESSOR RAMPOLE SOLVES A DELICATE
PROBLEM AT THE RIGHT MOMENT. A VENER-
ABLE TRADITION IS BY-PASSED FOR THE SECOND
TIME. BRITISH TEXTILE CIRCLES RECOVER THEIR
PEACE OF MIND.

WHEN Douglas learned of the hostile silence that had
greeted the judge's suggestion, and then that the Lord
Privy Seal had again asked Sir Arthur to his club, he
was gripped by a gnawing anxiety.

"They'll bungle the whole thing!" he said to Frances
with nervous apprehension.

"Who will?"

"The politicians," said Douglas. "I know them. Give
them the hardest crystal and they'll always turn out
a jellyfish in the end."

At the same hour, Sir Arthur was sitting amid the
fumed oak and dark red leather of a small room at the

Garrick Club, facing the Lord Privy Seal over a glass of old whisky.

"You upset them," said the minister.

"I gathered as much," said the judge. "But I fail to see how."

"You preach revolt, they say."

"What's that?"

"They don't like the idea that man is distinguished from the beast by his opposition to nature. How was it you put it? By his de-nature."

"Nobody contradicted me."

"Perhaps not, but they don't like it."

"It's not a question of liking or disliking it."

"Perhaps they couldn't immediately find a counter-argument. Though it seems to me that it might be objected . . . We are not really torn away from nature. We never shall be. We are part and parcel of it for good. Every cell in our body shouts aloud against your idea."

"Let them shout. That isn't what I said, either."

"I know, but . . ."

"We have torn ourselves away from nature as a man tears himself away from a crowd. He remains none the less part of the crowd, but he can look at it from outside, try to see clearly, escape from its hold."

"Possibly, possibly, but it doesn't sound good, don't you see. And besides, you'll be told too . . . don't you seem to treat nature as a stranger, not to say an enemy? But what would we do, what would we be, without her?"

"Why as an enemy? That word has some meaning for us, but not for nature."

"Perhaps. But all that doesn't sound good either. There would have to be too many explanations. You'd never

227

get the whole House to swallow . . . It's extraordinary enough that events have forced them to go so far, in spite of their horror of definitions. Don't make their task impossible. For that's the question, you know. You are perhaps right. I can't tell. It's outside my department. But in the eyes of the House you'll be wrong: that we may be sure of."

The judge took a large gulp of whisky to fortify his self-control.

"Whereas," went on the minister, "if we offer the House, with some acceptable explanations, an inviting definition . . . something that would shock nobody and suit them all . . ."

"But what?"

The minister studied the judge for a moment before saying:

"The spirit of religion."

The judge remained speechless.

"I have seen old Lord Humpty Dumpty," the minister continued with sudden volubility. "The whole Committee agrees. Even that rather fascist-minded young fellow, what's his name. Of course, you'd have to take the term "religion" in its widest sense. Religious spirit equals metaphysical spirit equals spirit of investigation, of restless inquiry, and so on. It could all be packed into it. Not only faith, but science, art, history, and also witchcraft, magic, the whole shoot. In short, it's all you said, in a way. Differently expressed, that's all."

"But," cried the judge, "the term is, to say the least, confoundedly ambiguous. It means nothing out of its context. It can even be used to mean the very opposite!"

The minister said with a smile:

228

"That's . . . hmm . . . just what's so convenient about it. . . ."

"In that case, what possible use do you expect the definition to be? You yourself, remember, referred to the Nuremberg laws. You yourself wished we could find a sufficiently solid basis on which to found an inviolable law for mankind. The religious spirit! How can we hope that Russia, for instance, would accept such a term, even if it's accompanied by all the explanations in the world! They might as well ask us to recognize the universal validity of Engels's definition, which is no less sound in its way. Should we do it?"

"My dear fellow," said the minister, "you're letting yourself be carried away. In theory, you may be a thousand times right. But in practice you will find that being right isn't worth a farthing in politics. We have an urgent problem to solve. It isn't a world problem, but a very modest problem that concerns the tropi people on the one hand, and our textile industry on the other. Man as a religious animal is a suggestion, as I told you, that would be acceptable to practically all members in the House. An incomplete definition, if you like. But is it a wrong one? No. Let us say it's a practical means of recognizing immediately whether or no the tropis have done what you say: torn themselves away from nature, claimed their independence, established their opposition, and all the rest of it. Isn't that right?"

"Ye-es . . . But as a matter of fact . . . I'm afraid the tropis have given no signs whatsoever of a spirit of religion. They don't even wear charms. . . ."

"I don't think that need worry us. . . . All in good time. I've also seen Professor Rampole. Some of his

229

observations, it seems, may come in very handy. So that particular problem may be solved quite speedily. Whereas if we try to get Parliament to approve a definition which is doubtless more complete, less equivocal, but which will start off endless debates, amendments, rejections, adjournments sine die, and what not, we'll never see the end of it. It would be of no help to anyone — neither to the tropis, to Templemore, to British justice, or even to your rights of man. Let's not take our bridges before we come to 'em, eh? We mustn't rush our fences, and all that. First things first: let's make do with what we can get — the rest will come in the fullness of time. You have the whole history of England to prove it to you."

Events did indeed confirm the Lord Privy Seal's forecasts.

On the basis of the Summer Committee's report, the House passed a bill, after various minor amendments, containing the following articles:

Section 1. Man is distinguished from the Beast by his spirit of religion.

Section 2. The principal signs of a spirit of religion are, in decreasing order of importance: faith in God, science, art and all its manifestations; the various religious creeds and philosophies and all their manifestations; ritual cannibalism and its manifestations.

Section 3. Any animate being that displays one or more of the signs mentioned in Section 2 is admitted to the human community, and its person protected throughout the United Kingdom, the British Commonwealth, and Her Majesty's colonies across the

230

seas, by the various provisions figuring in the last Declaration of the Rights of man.

As soon as the bill had become an act of Parliament, an M.P., known to have ties with the textile industry, asked what was going to be done about the tropis.

He was reminded that this question could not, in the view of the government, be as yet discussed in Parliament, since it might unduly affect the outcome of a pending lawsuit.

But the member protested vehemently against this view of the matter.

He asked whether, in the unimaginable event of Scotland, like Ireland, separating from the United Kingdom and claiming its independence, it would be held impossible to raise the Scottish question in Parliament until a pending action had been settled in Edinburgh against one MacTavish, prosecuted for insulting the Crown — although the decision taken in regard to Scottish independence would certainly exert a great influence on the fate of Mr. MacTavish?

He went on to say that the killing of an individual tropi was one thing, and the legal status of the tropis, as a whole, another, and that the latter could no more wait on the former than the fate of the United Kingdom on the trial of an individual Scotsman. It was on the contrary, he maintained, the duty of Parliament to settle a question that had proved pressing both from a purely humanitarian standpoint and from the economic and national point of view.

A member of the opposition objected that the last speaker's example was as irrelevant as it was inept. There was no comparison between the urgency of settling the status of a semibrute society and of debating the unity of the Kingdom. In addition, he asked, how could any legislation about the tropis, passed by the British Parliament, be in any way binding on Australia and New Guinea?

The first speaker reminded the House that Great Britain had, on many occasions, made its moral authority felt not only with the Dominions but with foreign nations as well, when some principle of humanity was too flagrantly flouted.

As regards the urgency, he said, could any feeling man declare "not urgent" the rescue of an entire people from the monstrous slavery with which it was threatened?

After a lively debate there was general support for a proposal that the terms of reference of the Summer Committee should be extended to include the defining of the tropis' nature. It was, however, agreed beforehand that the House was not competent to introduce legislation on the status of the tropis. Parliament would have to confine itself to a "recommendation" which would be submitted simultaneously to the United Nations Organization as well as to the Government of Australia and the Governor-General of New Guinea.

སྭ

The Committee, which Sir Peter Rampole had been invited to join in his capacity of an expert on primitive psychology, heard in turn Kreps, Pop, Willy, the Greames, and several other anthropologists who had been able to study the behavior of the tropis since their arrival in London.

It seemed at first that no sign of a spirit of religion could be detected in them. They made no use of fetishes,

232

amulets, tattooing, had no dances or rituals of any kind — let alone vestiges of art or science. Though they interred their dead, they did it as many animals do, and in the way that most animals bury their excrements, prompted by some atavistic instinct to avoid the dangers of decay or to cover up their tracks. No funerary rites whatsoever could be observed in use among the tropis.

They did not even show the slightest tendency towards cannibalism. They did not devour each other, nor had they ever been observed trying to lure or snare a human being with a view to devouring him. They had not even done so in the case of the Papuan porters, in spite of their immediate and obvious dislike of the latter.

Faced with these disappointing conclusions, the Committee asked Sir Peter to study once more all those statements with the greatest care, together with Sir Arthur, in the hope of extracting from them, if possible, some more encouraging symptoms. Sir Kenneth intimated to the psychologist, without being too explicit or suggesting, of course, the least tinkering with the evidence, that the discovery of some such sign was deemed eminently desirable.

At the next meeting, Sir Peter announced that a very significant point had, in fact, emerged from the statements which had been minutely sifted by Sir Arthur and himself.

"It concerns cannibalism," he said. "The practice of man-eating, even in those rare instances where its main aim is to satisfy hunger or gluttony, is always, in its essence, a ritual practice.

"It is regrettable, to be sure, that no tendency towards man-eating has been observed in the tropis.

233

"Luckily the Papuans did not show a similar restraint, with regard to the tropis. They ate them clandestinely on several occasions.

"We must specially note this fact: the Papuan orgies were clandestine.

"This being so, the Papuans must have wished either to conceal them from the white men, or to prevent the white men from watching the accompanying rites or ceremonies.

"Now, they would not have taken these precautions had they thought they were merely feasting on ordinary animal flesh. So we can suppose that they considered they were indulging in cannibalism, and eating not animals but human beings."

Sir Peter Rampole paused for a moment. Then he continued:

"That is merely a clue for us to follow. We obviously cannot trust the Papuans' instincts rather than the accuracy of six months' close observation of the tropis by a brilliant team of scientists.

"On the other hand, we are even less justified in ignoring this hint altogether. We must take into account the clue provided by the instinct of those men who are so much closer than we are to the primitive manifestations of the human mind, and who may thus detect, far better than we can, its first, faint signs in others.

"My opinion therefore is that we may have overlooked, or failed to identify, some exceedingly primitive sign of a spirit of religion, which did not escape the Papuans.

"Sir Arthur and I have some idea of what this may be. But for confirmation we should have to dig more deeply into certain statements made to the Committee."

234

He added that he thought these details could be obtained from his distinguished colleague, the geologist Professor Kreps, who had been able to bring to the study of the tropis a keenly scientific mind unhampered by a zoologist's or anthropologist's parochialism or prejudice. No testimony, he thought, could be more unbiased than his.

So Kreps was heard again at the next sitting.

Sir Peter asked him if the Papuans had attacked indiscriminately the cliff-dwelling tropis and those in the compound.

Kreps replied that they hadn't. The Papuan raiding parties had been confined to the cliffs. Rather an odd fact, he admitted, since the domestic tropis were far more conveniently within their reach. No special watch had been kept over the compound, he explained, at least in the early days, so that they would have been an easy prey.

Sir Peter then asked whether a great deal of smoked meat had been found in the caves during their first visits to the cliffs.

Kreps said that they had found only very little.

"We understood," said Sir Peter, "that the tropis smoked their meat in order to preserve it?"

"That's what we thought too, at first. However, we never actually found that they did preserve it. They went out hunting whenever there was need, and consumed their booty at once."

"Are you sure they smoked their meat without cooking it?"

"Oh, absolutely!" said Kreps. "We never managed to make our tropis eat the least morsel of cooked meat.

235

They loathe it. Their real treat is perfectly raw meat."

"Then why do they smoke it, if it's neither to preserve it nor because they like its taste?"

"To be perfectly frank, I have no idea. As a matter of
fact, something rather odd happened: the cliff tropis
never ate a scrap of meat that they hadn't left hanging
over the fire for at least a day. They did this even to
the ham we gave them, as if to make quite sure that it
was smoked according to the rules. Whereas those in
the compound greedily swallowed any raw meat we
gave them, without standing on ceremony."

"And you drew no conclusion from this?"

"Well, you know," said Kreps, "it's common enough
for captive animals to drop pretty quickly certain habits
of their wild life, even quite instinctive ones."

"However," said Sir Peter, "here are some facts that
are all strange in themselves, and even more so when
taken in conjunction.

"First, the tropis prefer their meat quite raw. Secondly,
the cliff tropis nevertheless carefully hang it over the
fire, but not in order to preserve it. Thirdly, the domestic
tropis promptly drop this practice. Fourth and lastly,
the Papuans indulge in cannibalistic orgies of the former,
and scorn the latter.

"Wasn't it you," he asked Kreps, "who said, talking
of the domestic tropis: 'We've scooped all the flunkeys'?"

"Yes, indeed," laughed Kreps.

"Let us now," said Sir Peter, "try to put ourselves in
the Papuans' place. They have there before them a
strange people — half ape, half human. Part of that people seem proud, jealous of their independence; they
indulge in a practice which the Papuans recognize, less

236

as instinct or preference, than as a very primitive fire worship, a homage paid to its magic power of purification and exorcism. The rest of the tropis, frivolous and carefree, renounce their liberty for a handful of raw meat. Left to themselves, they promptly abandon a practice which they had followed out of imitation and not by instinct — still less by reason. And our Papuans are not mistaken: they treat the former as men, the latter as apes.

"We believe that they are right. In this people on the borderline between man and beast, all have not equally crossed the line. But it is enough, to our mind, that some of them have crossed it for the entire species to be received within the human community."

"Besides," Sir Arthur confided later to Sir Kenneth, "how many of us would have the right to the title "man," if all of us had had to cross the borderline unaided? . . ."

The Summer Committee thus reported to Parliament that the tropis, having shown signs of a spirit of religion by a ritual practice of fire worship, should be admitted to the human community.

The report added that the state of extreme wildness in which this people lived suggested that they had need of protection against themselves as well as against outside interference. It recommended that their status should therefore be the subject of a special mandate to be entrusted to New Guinea and Australia, under the supervision of the United Nations.

These suggestions all received wide support, and the night after the vote in the House, a vast shiver of relief rose from the bosom of the great industrial family of British woolens.

237

Chapter 17

A PURELY FORMAL TRIAL. THE JURY'S RELIEF.
ALL SEEMS WELL THAT ENDS WELL. DOUGLAS
TEMPLEMORE'S DESPONDENCY. FRANCES DIS-
COVERS REASONS FOR HOPE AMID REASONS FOR
DESPAIR. MR. JUSTICE DRAPER CONTRADICTS HIM-
SELF WITH A SMILE. "THE AGE OF FUNDAMEN-
TALS HAS STARTED AGAIN." PROSPECTS OF HOPE
AT THE PROSPECT OF WHITBY.

THE second trial opened in an atmosphere no longer of
high passions, but of curiosity tinged with sympathy for
the accused. Now that everything was clear, the murder
became a murder like any other. The general wish was
that the accused should get off lightly, for his part in the
emancipation of the tropis was not forgotten. It was hoped
that the Crown would show itself sympathetic and the
jury merciful. Bets were made on the sentence the accused
would have to serve, some bold spirits even backing him
for an acquittal. The sums involved were substantial.

Lady Draper did her best to set Frances's mind at rest,

238

and could not understand why she was so downcast. The new judge, she assured her, was an old friend of her husband's. So was counsel for the prosecution. It was, of course, out of the question for Sir Arthur to seek to influence them, but he had at least been able to sound them as to their views. And these seemed to be favorable to the accused.

The trial did indeed pass off for the most part like a mere formality. There were few witnesses, as the only evidence needed was on the circumstances of the murder. The prosecution, as was expected, did not prove too severe. He said that a murder having been committed and now amply proved, it was out of the question to declare the accused not guilty. However, in view of the motive for the crime, and the fact that when it was committed the accused was unaware of the exact nature of the deceased, the Crown was prepared to admit the existence of extenuating circumstances.

Mr. Jameson, counsel for the defense, thanked the Crown for the understanding it had shown, but said that his learned friend had not gone far enough in the lesson he had drawn from the facts.

"The Crown recognizes," he said, "that at the time of the murder the accused was unaware of the deceased's true nature. But is that the proper way to put it? I do not think so.

"I contend that at the time of the murder the deceased was not a human being at all."

He paused for a moment after those words. Then he went on:

"In fact, special legislation was needed to define the

human being. And yet further legislation to include the tropis in that definition.

"This shows that it did not rest with the tropis to be or not to be members of the human community, *but with us to admit them to it*.

"It shows too that no one is a human being by a right of nature, but that, on the contrary, before being recognized as such by his fellow men, he must have undergone —in a manner of speaking — an examination, an initiation.

"Mankind resembles a very exclusive club. What we call human is defined by us alone. The rules within the club are valid for us alone. Hence the need for a legal basis to be established, as much for the admission of new members as for setting up rules and regulations applicable to all.

"It is obvious, therefore, that before being accepted as members, the tropis could not share in the life of the club nor claim the benefit of the club regulations.

"In other words, we could not demand of anyone that he should treat the tropis as human beings before we ourselves had decided that they were entitled to that appellation.

"To declare the accused guilty would thus be equivalent to applying the law retrospectively. As if, supposing a new regulation were introduced that compelled vehicles to keep to the right, a fine were then imposed on all drivers who had hitherto kept to the left.

"It would be a crying injustice, besides being profoundly contrary to the spirit of all our laws.

"The facts are clear.

240

"The tropis — thanks, incidentally, to the accused — have been legally admitted to the human community. They share the rights of man. They are no longer threatened. No other primitive or backward race, once jeopardized by the absence of any legal definition, is threatened any more.

"The jury therefore need have no qualms that the defendant's acquittal might have unfortunate consequences.

"On the other hand, you may be sure, ladies and gentlemen of the jury, that if you find the accused guilty, you will be responsible for a mistake, a misdeed, an appalling miscarriage of justice.

"For not only was the little victim as yet unrecognized as a human being at the time of its death, but it is common knowledge that its sacrifice lies at the root of the emancipation of all its people, as well as of a precious clarification of the laws of mankind in general.

"I therefore trust you to return a verdict fraught with wisdom and equity."

The judge's summing-up was genial. Though calmly impartial, he yet clearly showed that common sense favored the plea for the defense. The jury felt great relief. It retired for only a few minutes before bringing in, to the delight of the public, a verdict of *Not Guilty*.

∽

In the taxi that was taking them to dine at Lady Draper's, Douglas and Frances remained silent in each other's arms. At the sight of his weary face, there was nothing she dared say. And what could she have said? She felt too acutely that to Douglas, as to her, the whole

241

venture seemed to have petered out in half-failure rather than to have achieved a half victory.

Before their hosts, however, they both kept up an appearance of calm content. True to the unwritten law of custom, nobody referred at dinner to what was filling all their hearts. Hardly was the trial alluded to, and then only to compare the rival merits of the two counsels, not in the legal forum, but on the cricket field.

After dinner Lady Draper led Frances into the drawing room, while Sir Arthur and Douglas went into the study.

"You are not happy," said Lady Draper affectionately.

"Douglas has not succeeded," said Frances.

"That isn't what Arthur thinks."

"Isn't it?" asked Frances hopefully.

"Arthur is very pleased. He thinks that you have gained more than could be hoped. Mind you, my dear, I myself probably have different ideas about it from you. Douglas is free, and that is splendid. It's the main thing. But what an idea to have gone and stirred up all that!"

"Stirred up all what, Gertrude?" — they called each other by their Christian names now.

"Do you think the tropis will be any happier now they are human? I very much doubt it."

"They certainly won't be," said Frances.

"Ah! So you think as I do?"

"It is not a question of happiness," said Frances. "That word, I think, distorts everything."

"They lived a wonderfully carefree life. Now we'll have to start educating them, I suppose?" asked Gertrude with caustic pity.

"I suppose so," Frances agreed.

"They'll become liars, thieves — vain, selfish, mean
. . ."

"Maybe," said Frances.

"They'll start fighting and killing each other. Fine present we've given them, I must say."

"I think it is," said Frances.

"A fine present?"

"Yes, a very fine present. I've thought a lot about that lately, too. At first I was terribly sad."

"About the tropis?"

"No, about Douglas. He's been acquitted. But he's a murderer all the same, whatever they say."

"*You* think that?"

"I do. He has killed a baby, his son. With my complicity. All the legal quibbles won't alter that. At first I cried about it every night. I just had to bite my pillow. I remembered . . . a godfather I had when I was a little girl. He had a car. That was still quite rare in those days. I admired him, I adored him. One day Daddy told me . . . Godfather was in prison for a month. Some children had been playing hopscotch in a small street. He hadn't even realized at once that he had run over one of them. It was only when he got out of the car that he saw the little head sticking out from under the car . . . . They almost lynched him. "It wasn't his fault at all," Daddy told us. "You must love him as much as before." And I did love him as much. Only, when he came to see us afterwards, I felt a sort of horror . . . I was a little girl, of course . . . I couldn't help myself. It wouldn't be like that today. But nevertheless . . . I can't altogether help myself either

243

when I think of Douglas . . . . You think I'm horrible, don't you?"

"You surprise me a little," admitted Gertrude thoughtfully.

"*I* thought I was horrible. And then . . . now I think that it is right. Douglas explained to me why, one day. I've rather forgotten it now. But it *is* beautiful, I too feel it. This pain, this horror, that's the beauty of man. The animals must certainly be more happy, not feeling them. But I wouldn't for an empire change that pain and even that horror, and even our lies and selfishness and hate, for their unconsciousness, for their happiness."

Lady Draper murmured: "Neither would I, for that matter," and she remained sunk in thought.

"The case of the tropis has at least taught us one thing," said Frances. "Humanity is not a state we suffer. It's a dignity we must strive to win. A dignity full of pain and sorrow. Won, no doubt, at the price of tears. The tropis will have to shed them, with a lot of blood, and sound and fury. But now I know, I know that all this isn't 'a tale told by an idiot, signifying nothing.'"

"That's what I should have said to Douglas," she thought as she spoke. She thought too that you only find your own reasons when you are faced with the unreason of others.

"It's a fiasco," said Douglas bitterly, sipping his port.

"You have the uncompromising spirit of youth," said Sir Arthur. "Neck or nothing, eh?"

"But the little that has been done can't do any good and, what's more, it's only been done for sordid reasons.

244

That's even harder to bear than nothing at all."

"No, it's been done. That's the main thing. It's rather funny to hear myself talk like that," he added with a little grimace of self-mockery.

"I don't see why."

"You should have heard me argue with the Lord Privy Seal. I told him the very opposite."

"And now you have changed your mind?"

"Not at all. That's what's funny. With him I thought as you do. With you I think as he does. And if you come down to brass tacks, there is a precious lesson in all that."

"I wonder what?"

"I no longer remember," said the judge, "who wrote: 'it would be too beautiful to die for an entirely just cause.' The justice of even the best of causes is generally only a by-product. For effective support a cause always needs those interests which you call sordid. But now we know why, you and I. That very duality is part of the human condition. And far from its being our choice, it's against it that we are fighting. And so the dignity of men resides even in their failures, even in their falls."

"And what do I do next?" Douglas asked despondently.

"Why," said the judge, "you go on, of course!"

"What! Go on — killing tropis?"

"Good Lord, no!" cried Sir Arthur, and he laughed till the tears came. "Heavens alive, what an idea! What I meant was — you're still a writer, aren't you?"

With a smile he handed Douglas a batch of newspapers in which the passages to be read had been carefully marked by him in blue. They all dealt with the definition of man adopted by the United Kingdom, and expounded

245

by Sir Arthur in the columns of *The Times*. They all attacked it fiercely. None offered an alternative one. And the grounds on which it was opposed were as varied as the flowers in a midsummer garden.

A French parliamentarian, asked by a reporter what he thought of this new piece of legislation, said that "his feelings towards his British colleagues were too friendly for him to wish to talk about it." This made Douglas laugh. "What a cat!" he said. "Why the devil doesn't he explain his reasons for disagreeing!"

"Because he can't, no doubt," said the judge.

"Why not?"

"That's the point I tried to make in my article: the mere existence of disagreement is the first proof that, on the one hand, ultimate truth is denied us — else how could we disagree? — and on the other, that we go on seeking it — else why argue about it? Yet that is what the law, however ambiguous and incomplete it may be, expresses after all. Now how can anyone contest that argument without automatically providing added proof of it?"

"But, surely, that fellow knows it?"

"Probably not. Most of these disagreements, you'll see, spring from sentimental reasons or from intellectual prejudices. You'll never find them supported by any logical argument — and for a good reason. But the mind has a wonderful knack of brushing aside whatever irks it, without resorting to reason."

. . . A long time ago [Douglas read in the *Welsh Worker*] Marx and Engels went to much trouble to prove that man is defined by the transformations he has imposed on nature. Our loyal Commons, who

246

are by no means Communists, have taken great pains to be differently of the same opinion. Let's take note of their good intentions, but point out to them in all friendship that they are throwing the door wide open to dangerous errors.

"But he doesn't explain why, either," chuckled Douglas. Another article said:

This notion of the spirit of religion could be useful and fertile provided it is taken in its widest sense. But it is the product of a political gathering and that alone serves to deprive it of all value in our eyes.

"That's fantastic!" exclaimed Douglas. "It's question of whether the definition is right, wrong, or inadequate, not of knowing whether the author . . ."

"Don't upset yourself!" said Sir Arthur. "That sort of dishonesty we can all fall into at times."

But Douglas was already laughing over another article:

This notion of the spirit of religion, provided it were limited to the Christian faith, might possibly be admitted if . . .

"It makes you despair."

"Not at all," said Sir Arthur. "Not at all. And think what it would have been like if we'd tried to obtain a more complete definition at once — the wrench, the refusal, the fight, the de-nature!"

"We'll never get there," said Douglas.

"We will in time — if the definition holds true," said Sir Arthur. "Truth always takes longest to triumph — very understandably so. But it does triumph in the end.

247

Still, that isn't the most essential thing, in point of fact."

"What on earth is, then?"

"It's what you have done, my boy," said Sir Arthur. "You've disturbed people. You've made them sit up and face an incredible gap that's been there for thousands of years. What Frenchman was it wrote not so long ago: 'Reason must be built on fresh foundations. The age of fundamentals has started again.' You have shown that this is true, that everything had been built on air. That much people have grasped, they have gone and attended to the most pressing need, they've stopped the gap as best they could. It still remains to be done better and more completely. And that won't happen without much gnashing of teeth. But you've set the ball rolling, it's a pretty big ball, nothing can stop it any more."

As a last plum, Sir Arthur gave Douglas an article published in *Gargoyle*, a literary magazine. The author, well known for his linguistic studies, wrote:

It is high time that the last be heard of that inane tropi affair. What could be more depressing than the sight of so many first-rate intellects wasting their time (and acumen) on problems as footling, false and fruitless as a definition of man? Thank goodness, that is over: may we hear no more about it! Instead, I suggest, we should return to serious matters. And just in time, too: for an extraordinary (autobiographical) novel has just come out which has the right to claim our unimpaired seriousness. I entreat you to read it. The (anonymous) author describes how, when as an adolescent he strangled his mother in order to rob (or rape) her, words suddenly under-

248

went (in his psyche) a magical distortion which imediately assumed a sacred quality. Thus plunged into the mysteries of a vibrantly new and intense vocabulary, we are carried away into a labyrinth of breath-taking obscenities in which the mind (losing its footing at every turn) discovers, in a sort of quintessential mystification, the brittle meaning of existence itself.

Might one not say that man is defined by this debilitating pursuit (of impalpable myths)? How else can one explain . . .

Douglas raised his head. All trace of weariness had vanished from his face. He looked at Sir Arthur with a broad, relaxed, affectionate grin. When Gertrude and Frances joined them a little later, the two men were still chuckling contentedly.

And Douglas, yielding to a sudden impulse, took them all along to plunge themselves for an hour in the jostling, smoky atmosphere of The Prospect of Whitby, where the music and the songs, the wild and wonderful medley of gewgaws, the mummified head, the souvenirs of the sea, of weddings and disasters, of games, of business, of adventure, were so many joyful tokens of man's love for this enfranchised world that he has created in his own image.